# THE CLEANSING

# The Cleansing

CAL NEUBERT

## ~ 1 ~

It was a rainy night in Portland, Oregon, just like usual. The clouds were low and hid the tops of the skyscrapers. A dense fog was dodging its way between the buildings as a middle-aged man was walking home from work.

His name was Patrick Hopkins. He stood about five foot eleven and was well put together. It was around 10:00 p.m., and he was coming home from a late night at work. He usually took the bus, but that night the 9:30 didn't show, so he decided to walk home.

He lived about fifteen minutes away by bus, so he had a good forty-five minutes to walk. He asked his phone for directions, and it told him he could take a shortcut if he went under the overpass on the west side of the city. He headed in that direction.

It took him a few minutes, but he reached the overpass and began to look around. It was a quiet night. Nobody was on the road. Everyone had gone home. The streetlights were barely lighting the street, and the only thing he could hear was the sound of the rain lightly tapping the roads and buildings of the surrounding city. He looked up for a moment and took a deep breath and felt relaxed. After a minute or two, he continued to walk down the dimly lit street.

Under the overpass now, the feeling of calmness suddenly faded. The buildings became broken and abandoned. Trash and glass filled the alleyways between each structure. The buildings that weren't abandoned had neon signs that flickered on and off, reflecting colored light off the raindrops.

After a while, Patrick felt something strange. A shocking sensation traveled down his spine, triggering all his senses to heighten. He turned to notice a building that gave him an awful feeling, one that made him aware of the burbling bile that was brewing in his stomach.

It was an old chapel. The cross was missing, but it was easily identifiable due to the way the building was shaped. The windows all around it were boarded up, and it was covered in darkness—or maybe it seemed that way because it looked as though it had been burned by fire.

Chills now covering his whole body, Patrick began to feel his sweat mix in with the raindrops already on his face. He felt as if he was being watched from a small crack between the boarded-up windows of the chapel. His heart filled with fear, and the only action he could think of was to get away from that building as soon as possible.

But before he took his eyes away, he noticed something coming from the chapel. A faint light, a candle maybe, shined between the cracks—it was moving around. Someone was in there. Patrick instantly dropped his stuff, including his umbrella, and he ran away as fast as possible. He didn't know why it scared him so much, but the vibe of that entire area just felt...sick.

Sprinting like his life depended on it, Patrick panted and moved his legs as fast as he could. He had no regard for his speed or where he was going. As he ran like a bat out of hell, he became further and further lost.

He stopped at a street corner to catch his breath. At one point, he swallowed the mucus that had risen to his throat. He was struggling. He was in shape, but the fear was killing him.

He briefly looked across the street. His eyes kept surveying the area, but he had to do a double take, because across the street and under a streetlight was a tall figure—very tall. Very, very tall. About six foot ten and covered in black robes. It had what looked like a sack on its head. Patrick's eyes went wide.

The two looked at each other for a long while. Doing absolutely nothing. Just watching one another. Then, slowly, the being raised its arm up until its elbow made a ninety-degree angle, and, ever so slowly, it started moving its hand back and forth.

It was waving.

Something about that wave sent Patrick over the edge. In a normal setting, he would've asked if the man was okay. But at that moment, the way both his body and mind felt, he wasn't taking any chances. He took a step forward, but the second he did, he heard a strange noise coming from across the street. A gasping, almost choking noise that stopped Patrick in his tracks.

He slowly glanced back at the being, whose hand had stopped waving. After a short while, its hand slowly returned to its side. Scared beyond belief, Patrick turned around and started walking away from the masked stranger.

He walked a few steps until, amid the sound of rain hitting concrete, he heard faint but quick footsteps followed by another gasping sound. Patrick quickly turned around. The tall being was now on his side of the street. It stood still under a street lamp maybe twenty yards from Patrick.

He mumbled to himself, "Not me. Not today. No, no, no," and started backing up as he glanced behind him to make sure he was still going the right way.

*BAM!*

The being slammed its foot on the ground in order to keep Patrick's attention. Then the tall figure sat still for a moment. Patrick stared at the being, and the being stared back at him, although the weird brown potato-like sack didn't allow any sort of emotion. Just two little holes where only darkness could be seen.

All of a sudden, the tall figure began to sway back and forth in a dancing motion. The long, almost sticklike arms of the being rose and swayed with the rest of its body. Patrick, frozen by fear, wasn't sure what to do.

The being continued to dance closer and closer.

Every time Patrick would attempt to take his eyes off the thing closing in on him, another gasp from the creature would freeze him with fear. Before he knew it, the being was only a couple feet in front of him. Patrick screamed as the streetlight flickered off.

# ~ 2 ~

That same night, at around 10:00 p.m. over at Portland University, a decent sized college campus in the city of Portland, a psychology professor named Lewis Nelson was alone in his office, grading papers.

With only one small lamp turned on, his office was quite dark. The lamp, however, lit up the papers just enough to where he could see what he was doing. Lewis was a newer teacher, but a bright mind at that. He was in his mid-thirties and taught criminology to students who wanted to step into the minds of serial killers and learn about how the criminal justice system handles people like that.

He sat in silence as he reread the grade he'd given the sophomore Tessa Jameson. She was one of those students who always came to class with a smile and was ready to learn. Obviously, she was one of the smartest in the class.

Lewis read the title of her paper: "Be Careful of What the Mind Can Do." The paper he'd assigned to the class was supposed to demonstrate how powerful the mind can be. The lesson included a lecture on how the mind, if it wants something enough, can bend reality at its will.

Most of the papers used examples of good things the mind can do. For example, one student used the "mom lifts car off of baby" story. And, while Lewis acknowledged in class that that was correct, he was looking for something a little deeper.

Tessa's paper, however, talked about how people can train their mind to do powerful things, like learning how to be closer with nature through meditation or get closer to a God by using prayer. But some train their minds for all of the wrong reasons. Tessa's paper went on to discuss how some serial killers consider themselves the good guys because they might see the world as overpopulated. She mentioned that some get the twisted idea that they are carrying out the Lord's will. And when a person believes the horrible things they do are for the good of somebody else, it is truly danger-ous and almost impossible to stop them.

Lewis smiled as he put an A on Tessa's paper. He then proceeded to put the rest of the graded papers into his drawer and the ungraded ones into his brown leather brief-case. He sighed as he got up from his chair and took his black sports coat off the coat hanger right next to his desk. He threw it over his shoulders and walked out the door, locking it behind him.

Lewis walked down the hallway whistling the tune of a student's ringtone that went off earlier in class until he got to a door that was lit up green by the exit sign that sat above it. As he walked out of the psychology building, he grabbed his umbrella and lifted it above his head to shield himself from the rain.

About 10:10 now, and Lewis was walking to his car. Listening to the rain around him, he pulled his keys out from his pocket and clicked the unlock button. A gray Prius in the distance gave a brief response. As he got to his car, Lewis collapsed his umbrella, opened the door, threw his belongings onto the passenger side seat, and pushed the button that started the car.

He reached over and turned the radio on. He sat back and began to drive out of the parking lot. His favorite radio station was basically a talk show in which the host had listeners call in and talk about crazy conspiracies. The host of the show, Ron Stevens, had a deep and soothing voice.

And, while the majority of the stories were obviously fake, there were some that were interesting and sparked Lewis' imagination and curiosity. He often took ideas from the show and used them in his lectures if they made enough sense.

"Next up, we have Jason," Ron Stevens began in a low tone, "who claims he was able to achieve astral projection."

The streetlight in front of Lewis turned yellow, and he began to slow down. He came to a complete stop as he laughed at what he had just heard over the radio. But he continued to listen.

"Jason what do you have for us?" Ron asked.

There was a bit of static, then a small voice came on. Lewis envisioned a skinny, thirty-five-year-old man who lived in his parents' basement and was just looking for attention.

Jason began to talk. "Yeah, hi, so basically I wanted to start off by saying that I'm a huge fan of the show." His voice was shaking a bit.

Ron cut the guy off instantly and said, "Thank you, Jason. So, what's this about astral projection?"

"Oh, oh, yeah," Jason said. After a brief pause, he continued. "Well, one time I was in my mom's basement..."

Lewis gave himself a nod, as though he'd drained a three-pointer in a basketball game. The light turned green, and he began driving as Jason continued.

"Well, one second I was there, and the next I was upstairs."

Nearing an underpass and another stoplight, Lewis noticed one of the streetlights was off, which made that particular corner as black as the night sky. He noticed something to his left but couldn't make it out immediately.

It was as if there was a dark streak of something on the sidewalk. It looked like a paint stroke. At least, that's what Lewis told himself it was as the light turned green and he proceeded to turn right, toward home. He looked in his rearview mirror and saw nothing except the flicker of the streetlight. He continued to listen to Jason on the radio, who eventually came to the realization on air that he was probably just high.

When Lewis arrived at his small suburban house outside the city, he opened up his garage door and drove in. It was about 10:30 p.m. now, and he unpacked his belongings from the car and headed inside. As he entered, he hung his coat up on its hanger by the front door, kicked off his shoes, and was greeted by his eleven-year-old German shepherd, Apollo.

"Hi, buddy," Lewis said while petting his dog between the ears. Apollo let out a large groan, and Lewis replied, "Yeah, same here, bud."

While chuckling, Lewis headed to his office and threw his bags inside. He turned around and walked to his bedroom. The TV was on, and his wife Karissa was sound asleep, her brown hair spread out across the pillow.

He was quiet as he entered, whispering to Apollo to come in. Apollo trotted through the doorway and headed straight to his bed in the corner and sat down. Lewis went into his bathroom and changed into his nighttime clothes, which included a white tank top and gym shorts.

He sat there for a second and looked at himself in the mirror. Lewis had dark brown hair that was usually styled to look like a wave. He had a scruffy beard that he would trim nearly every day before it got out of hand. He was slim but had some muscle definition as well. But not much.

After he was done inspecting the signs of aging, he brushed his teeth and turned off the light before leaving the bathroom. He quietly climbed into bed, trying not to wake up Karissa. He leaned over and kissed her on the forehead, then proceeded to grab the remote and turn off the TV before he dozed off into a deep sleep.

*

The next morning, Lewis awoke to Karissa kissing him on the head and telling him to wake up.

"Good morning, Lewy," she said playfully. "I made coffee."

As he did every morning, Lewis looked turned over and looked out the window next to his side of the bed. It allowed a sense of calmness, and it gave him the knowledge of the weather for the upcoming day.

He then got out of bed and replied as he received a cup, "Oh, you're amazing, honey, thank you." He took a sip. "What would I ever do without you?"

"Probably be homeless," she said while laughing. Karissa was dressed in a black pantsuit; her brown hair was wavy, and her white skin glistened. She was glowing.

"What's with the fancy getup today?" Lewis asked.

"Today is the day I talk to Jerry about the Griffin story," she said.

"Oh, I get it," he said. He got up and wrapped his arms around her stomach while she checked herself again in the mirror. "You're going to use your *astonishing* beauty to get your boss to give you that massive story that will one hundred percent put you in the big leagues."

She looked at him in the mirror. "Yeah, that's exactly right," she said.

They both laughed.

*

Lewis, now dressed in his work clothes and out in the kitchen, was feeding Apollo while watching the news like he did every morning. The old dog took a break from his food when he heard Karissa's high heels on the hardwood floor get louder and louder. He then shoved his face right back into his food bowl.

Karissa walked into the kitchen adjusting one of her earrings. Lewis looked over at her. "Oh, mama!" he said with a huge grin.

She looked over at him, blushing. "Stop it!" She said. He wrapped his arms around her waist, and she put hers over his shoulders. He leaned in for a kiss.

"I'm married to easily the best goddamn reporter this town has ever seen," he said, completely amazed at her beauty.

"I'm not sure that's true, because I have only been given stories about dog shows and Christmas pageants, but thank you," she said with a smile.

"Hey, you walk in there today, straight up walk into that man's office, and demand that story," Lewis replied. "You deserve it."

She looked up into his eyes and gave him a kiss. "You are my home, Lewis Nelson." They kissed again. They were eventually interrupted by a message on TV that caught both of their attentions.

"We now go live to Portland, Oregon, to bring you some shocking news."

Both of the Nelsons' grins morphed into curious expressions as they turned toward their television.

"The body of Portland native Patrick Hopkins was found dead this morning on the corner of Thirteenth and Grand Hill near downtown in what police have now confirmed is a homicide."

Karissa said in a very shallow voice, "I gotta go to work." She turned around, gave her husband a final kiss on the cheek, and walked out the front door.

Lewis stood there shocked as the anchors began to describe the scene.

"What you are about to witness is extremely graphic. Viewer discretion is advised."

A video popped up. It was obviously taken from the phone of a pedestrian who happened to walk by the crime scene before any law enforcement arrived. The video began by looking at the sidewalk for a few seconds. The audio was cut out so that the anchors could describe what everyone was seeing. Then, suddenly, the camera flipped up, abruptly showing a giant red blur.

They cut the video short, but the anchors said the body had been cut to pieces, as if Patrick Hopkins was mauled by a lion. They then went on to say that investigators believed it happened late at night and that the body would be sent in for an autopsy.

Lewis was instantly reminded of the night before. He was at that intersection. He now realized what that dark streak of paint on the sidewalk could've been.

"Truly disgusting," one anchor said. "Police are searching for a suspect who is around seven feet tall and wearing all black clothes, including what looked to be a mask of some sort covering his face."

Still frozen with shock, Lewis wondered what might've happened if he'd turned left instead of right at that intersection. Would he have been another victim of this killer? He turned off the TV and proceeded to grab his briefcase.

He thought to himself, *What if I could've helped? Maybe I could've done something, anything!* He threw on his coat and walked out the door without even saying goodbye to Apollo.

\*

The entire journey to campus, Lewis continued to ask himself if he could have done something to help the man who was brutally murdered the night before. After some time, he arrived at the stoplight under the overpass where he'd spotted the dark paint streak that he now knew was blood.

Police cars were still blocking off that side of the road. There were a few different news vans from multiple stations lined up on the street as well.

When the light turned green, Lewis kept driving while also gluing his eyes to the scene. Two police officers holding large shotguns stared at him as he drove by, and they continued to stare at him until he was out of their eyesight. Lewis' spine rattled with chills. He couldn't help but feel as though something was off about the whole thing.

*

Lewis was a few minutes late to class.

"Thank you all for staying; I'm sorry I'm a bit late," he said to the class. "Now, last class we were talking about Ted Bundy. Why do you guys think—"

He was cut off by one of his students in the front. "Mr. Nelson, are we seriously not going to talk about what happened last night?"

A few of the other students agreed.

"No. The man was murdered, and we should give it at least a few days before we talk about it like it will teach us something," Lewis replied, annoyed.

"But Mr. Nelson!" another student said.

"NO!" Lewis yelled while hitting his desk.

The students sat up straight and stopped their whispers and talking immediately. Lewis felt a strange tingle in the back of his spine. He sighed after a brief moment and said, "I am sorry, everybody."

He looked down at his desk and continued, "It was a long night, and this murder just got to me for some reason. We will talk about it in the near future, but until they have all of the facts as to why someone would kill Mr. Hopkins, we will continue with our regularly scheduled lectures, okay?"

Everyone nodded in agreement, and Lewis continued the lecture about Ted Bundy until the end of class an hour later.

After class ended, Tessa Jameson walked up to Lewis' desk while her other classmates walked out in a hurry. She stood in front of him while he was packing his things into his briefcase. Without looking at her, he said, "What is it, Tessa? I gotta go."

"I know," she explained, "but I was just curious what you thought of my paper."

Lewis stopped packing his things and looked at her. "How do *you* think you did?" he asked.

She looked disappointed, as that was obviously not the answer she was looking for.

"Tessa, I really enjoyed it," he said with a smirk.

Tessa looked at him with excitement.

"Between you and me," he started, "this is exactly what I was looking for."

Her smile grew larger.

"Most of the class used this paper to explain how the mind is the most powerful tool—which was the goal. But they used only positive examples. Your idea that serial killers sometimes have deranged ideas about things like religion, and that those ideas can be held onto as tightly as if their child were stuck under a car and *that* is what allows them to perform these horrific tasks so easily is terrific."

Tessa smiled from ear to ear. "Thanks, Mr. Nelson!" she said as she trotted out of class.

When she opened the door, Jack Garcia, the dean of the school and also a good friend of the Nelsons, walked in with two men in black suits.

Lewis looked at them, troubled.

Jack approached and said, "Lewis, I need you to come with me."

"Is everything all right?" Lewis asked, confused.

Jack looked at him and sighed, "That's what we're going to find out."

Lewis followed Jack and the two men in suits to his office. After a few moments of silence, he asked, "Jack, what the hell is this? What's going on?"

Nobody responded to him. He knew it was serious, though, because Jack was coming to get him. Jack never asked Lewis to his office unless it was about their fantasy football league. And Jack's wife Lisa was very good friends with Karissa. Pretty much every Sunday during the fall, the families would get together and watch football games.

As they entered the office, a man was sitting at Jack's chair. He was wearing a black suit was tall and strong. He had blonde hair and matched it with a pretty large beard. He had a gun and a badge attached to his belt.

"What is this?" Lewis asked.

"Hello, Mr. Nelson. My name is Detective Bolton with the FBI, and I need to ask you a few questions. Please, sit," Bolton said, gesturing to the chair. The situation itself was strange, and it was especially strange with all the men in suits standing around, but Bolton's voice was nice and welcoming.

Lewis felt a little safer and more at ease after hearing the kindness in Bolton's voice. He was obviously a charming guy. They both sat down, and the detective gave Jack a kind smile. "Thank you, Mr. Garcia," he said.

Jack nodded and walked out. Now Lewis was nervous again. He was alone in a room full of FBI agents.

"Now," Detective Bolton said, putting his attention back onto Lewis. "I don't have a lot of time, and I know you don't either, so let's get through this, okay?"

"Yeah, well, what exactly is *this?*" Lewis asked nervously.

"Mr. Lewis Nelson. I'm sure you are aware of the events that transpired last night at Thirteenth and Grand Hill." Lewis nodded his head slowly. "Well, we were able to find a few things that pointed us in your direction. You might actually be able to help us."

"You think I was involved?" Lewis said loudly.

"Mr. Nelson, that's not what we were going to ask you," Bolton said. Then he took a long pause. "We were able to look at the traffic cameras from last night. At approximately 10:15 p.m., these images were taken."

Bolton pulled out a manila folder and opened it, taking out a few different pictures. Each was a screenshot from different traffic cameras at the street corner. They were all different angles, but one thing was clear: in every picture, Lewis' car was stopped at the light, and, only a few feet away from him, waiting in the darkness, was the tall man.

And when Lewis looked at the photographs, he was truly terrified. The pictures showed that his head was turned toward the street, where the dark streak was. And, if you looked past the streak, a figure in the dark was looking right at him. The photos looked as if Lewis and the tall figure were staring at each other. Chills went through his body.

"As you can see, Mr. Nelson," Bolton explained, "you were seen only feet away from the suspect last night, and we were wondering if you have any information about him."

"I didn't even see him standing there, honestly," Lewis replied. "I noticed a dark streak of something. I thought it was oil because it wasn't mixing with the rain, but all of my attention was on that, so I had no idea that freak was only a few feet from me." He paused. "He could've killed me right then and there. He could've followed me home. I could have led him to my wife."

Bolton's eyes widened a bit. "It's okay," he replied. "You're not in trouble or anything, Mr. Nelson. And as far as we know, he took off. We can have an officer or two put outside you house, if that will make you feel better."

The professor itched his wrist. "You guys don't have any leads?"

"Well, that's why we're here asking you. Because any information would help, and it seems that you were the closest to him," Bolton said, scratching his beard.

"But I mean, there aren't many people who are that tall, so he can't hide for long, right?" Lewis asked.

"Well, that's what we're hoping. I mean, it certainly narrows down the suspect list," Bolton replied.

"I'm sorry, guys," Lewis said, looking between the two detectives. "I wish I could be of more help."

"That's all right, Mr. Nelson. We appreciate your time," said Bolton.

Lewis got up and shook the detective's hand. "I don't think it's necessary to put officers outside my house. I mean, you guys can keep your eyes on us, but I don't want to scare my wife, and I also believe that every officer you guys have, you should be able to find this guy."

Bolton nodded his head, and Lewis walked out of the room. He went back to his classroom to get ready for his next lecture. As he sat down, he pulled out his phone. He had two messages from Karissa.

*Hey, babe, are you okay? This is crazy.*

*Jerry gave me the story! I'll have it up by lunch. How are you?*

At that moment, Lewis' heart was filled with joy. He knew how hard Karissa had worked to be a journalist, and she felt like this "Griffin story" was her key to the top.

Karissa had started out as an assistant for her boss, Jerry. She wanted to be a writer, but every time she came in with suggestions for stories, he turned her down. After two years of bringing in coffee and answering calls, she was offered the job of journalist on small stories. Ever since, she'd been begging for something big, and it seemed she just got it.

The joy in his heart quickly faded as he saw students beginning to walk into his classroom. He put his phone away and greeted them. At that moment, he felt an itch in his throat. A tingle in his brain. A scratching at his skull.

He shook his head and began his lecture.

# ~ 3 ~

Later that evening, Karissa walked through the door and was greeted by dinner and a bouquet of red roses.

"Hey! There she is! Congratulations, baby!" Lewis said while stepping up to give her a hug and a kiss. He was in his white dress shirt with the top button undone.

"Thank you, Lewy," she said. chuckling. "Oh, wow, you made dinner?"

"Of course I did; we gotta celebrate your story, K," Lewis said happily. The smell of chicken, rice, and vegetables filled the air.

Lewis put the food onto two white plates and drizzled the top with teriyaki sauce. He laid the plates out on the dinner table while Karissa filled up Apollo's food and water bowls. They both sat down and began to eat the stir fry that Lewis had prepared.

Apollo obviously had no interest in his dry dog food, as he ignored it and began to beg for some of the Nelsons' dinner.

"Oh, I almost forgot, I picked something up. I'll be right back," Lewis said excitedly.

Karissa watched him run into the garage. She then looked down at Apollo and snuck him a little piece of chicken, which he enjoyed very much.

Lewis came back into the kitchen with a large wine bottle.

"Oh, wow, look at you," Karissa said, smiling.

"We're going to pop this bad boy open, and you're going to tell me about your day!" he said while getting two wine-glasses from the kitchen. "So, how'd you manage to get this story from Jerry?" He was filling the glasses and walking them over to the table.

"Thanks baby," Karissa said, and then, taking a sip, "It just sort of happened. I walked in and was fully focused on the Griffin story. I didn't talk about anything else, and during our morning staff meeting, he gave it to me."

She took another sip and looked down at her food. "I guess," she started, her tone now sad and low, "I realize now that he only gave me the Griffin story because the reporter he assigned it to first was put on the Patrick Hopkins case."

Lewis looked at her with a glowing smile. "Hey."

She looked up from her dinner.

"I am so damn proud of you," he said before getting lost in her eyes. "The Griffin story is a big one! You were given an opportunity, and I know you're going to kill it."

She looked at his big brown eyes and smiled. "You're right," she said while her smile got bigger and bigger. "What about you?" Karissa asked, bringing Lewis out of his trance. "How was your day?"

As soon as she asked that, Lewis' entire demeanor changed. He slouched forward and spoke strangely. "Uh...it was...good," he said nervously.

She knew something was off.

"What happened? What is it?" she asked, concerned.

Lewis decided not to tell her about Bolton, although he didn't know why. He told his wife everything, and something major happened at work and he decided not to. It wasn't like he didn't want to. But he couldn't physically get the words out of his mouth.

"Nothing, K. Everybody was just a little shaken up, is all. There was even talk about cancelling classes earlier today." He began to stare into his wineglass. His eyes were examining its darkness. Something about it reminded him of the dark streak he saw on the sidewalk. And he was now aware that there was somebody watching him examine the dark streak of blood last night.

Karissa raised her eyebrows with worry and watched him get lost in the maroon liquid, until eventually things got back to normal and she changed the subject.

Around 8:00 p.m., Lewis and Karissa began to put the dishes away. While they laughed and played with Apollo, there was something lurking outside. Something in the shadows.

There was a figure. It was standing about ten feet away from their back window, which was partially covered by a tree.

And it wasn't eagerly looking in—no, it was just standing there. So still, so tall, it seemed like a tree itself. It stood there in the open, like it wouldn't care if somebody noticed it.

By 11:00 p.m., inside the house, only one light remained on in the kitchen. Karissa was sitting on the counter with her legs wrapped around Lewis' torso. They were kissing over and over again.

The being outside hadn't moved.

Lewis picked up Karissa and carried her into their bedroom. She laughed, and the being watched them shut the door.

That's when it moved.

It went around the house by their bedroom and stood a few feet from Lewis' bedside window. No tree in the way this time. Just the tall figure and the fence behind it that separated the Nelsons' house from their neighbors.

Lewis kissed Karissa's neck, and she turned her head toward the window. Her eyes closed as she moaned. After a brief moment, she opened them slowly and saw the being with its face pushed against the glass. Karissa screamed.

The being's face was as pale as a fresh blanket of snow but covered in dark red blood streams. Its eyes were almost popping out of its head, as it appeared it did not have eyelids. Its mouth was cut into a smile, which showed bloodstained yellow teeth that looked like corn kernels. It made a loud noise that sounded like somebody choking.

Lewis jumped off Karissa immediately as she kept screaming.

The professor yelled, "What the hell?!" Seeing his wife's eyes wide and glued to that window, he turned and looked in that direction and saw the shadow of something moving. On the window, he saw a very large bloodstained handprint.

Without time to think, Lewis yelled, "Call the cops!" He went into his closet, reached up onto the top shelf, and pulled out a large .44 Magnum revolver. He checked to make sure it was loaded.

After he grabbed it, he ran out into the living room. He yelled for Apollo to come with, but there was no sign of him. Lewis didn't even throw on his shoes, he just ran out onto the pavement and was shocked at what he saw.

At the end of the street stood a tall figure. It was under a streetlight and staring back at Lewis. "You son of a bitch! I'll kill you!" Lewis screamed with rage. Then, flashing blue and red lights began to light up around the tall being. The professor looked at the police cars as they arrived, but when he looked back to where the figure had been standing, it was gone. Lewis remained there, sweating profusely and breathing heavily. His eyes were wide open. An itch returned to his brain.

*

The police were inspecting the Nelsons' house. Their neighbors were outside in their bathrobes and pajamas. Karissa had come outside, and she was sitting on the front lawn with Lewis while the police did their job. She was wrapped up in his arms, sobbing.

A black SUV pulled up, and Detective Andrew Bolton stepped out, wearing a bulletproof vest with "FBI" written in yellow on the front. He greeted the couple.

"Lewis."

Before he could say anything else, Lewis looked down at his wife with great worry.

Bolton kneeled down and looked at Karissa. "You must be Mrs. Nelson. I'm sorry we had to meet under these conditions, but it's a pleasure. I'm Detective Bolton. I'm here to help you, but I need to understand what happened. Do you think you can help me understand?"

His voice was soothing. She stuttered a bit but began to tell him.

Lewis was lost in his own head. Somebody had come to his house and was on his property. There was a bloodstained handprint on his window.

Whose blood?

He came out of it when he heard Karissa say she could see the figure's face. She described it as "a face without skin."

She was obviously scared beyond belief.

*Who is he?*

*WHAT is he?*

Lewis thought again to the other night, at the stoplight. There was no doubt it was the same man.

Then an officer came up to Bolton and said, "We found a body."

Lewis realized who the body was. He held onto Karissa and started to cry. She looked at him and said, "Is it..."

And Lewis nodded his head, sobbing.

Bolton, confused, asked, "Who else was in the house?"

The officer said, "It's a dog, sir."

The Nelsons' sobbing got louder. Apollo was like a kid to them. He was part of the family. Bolton put his hand up to the officer and waved it, as if to say, *That's enough.* The officer nodded and walked away.

Bolton leaned over to the couple and said soothingly, "I think it'd be best for you guys to sleep somewhere else tonight. We'll clean up the house and make sure everything is ready for you to come back tomorrow. Here's my number. Call me if you need anything." He pulled out a card with his name and number on it and handed it to Lewis.

As Bolton was saying this, three police cars flew down the street, and static came over Bolton's radio. Lewis couldn't make out what it was saying, although it sounded urgent.

"I think we got him! I'll be in touch," Bolton said, then immediately sprinted back to his black SUV. Another police car pulled out after Bolton.

The Nelsons continued to sit there, in awe of the events that had occurred.

And as another officer approached Lewis and Karissa to ask about where they would be staying and offer police protection, Detective Bolton was on the move.

Over the radio in Bolton's car, an officer said, "Suspect was spotted heading northbound, wearing all black..."

Bolton reached over to his shoulder, where his radio hung, and interrupted, "He's a tall bastard; you can't miss him!" He slammed the gas pedal as far to the floor as it could go. "We need to catch this guy! Keep all eyes open!" he exclaimed.

Bolton turned out of the Nelsons' suburban neighborhood and onto a hill that led straight to downtown. "Where is he, goddamn it?!" Bolton screamed into the radio.

"Suspect spotted on Fremont Bridge," said an officer over the radio.

"Good, cut him off!" Bolton yelled as he turned his car around and headed straight there.

By the time Bolton got to the bridge, three police cars had corned the tall man near the center. The detective halted his car to a complete stop. He got out and started toward the standoff. He passed another officer, who said, "Detective, wait until you see the shape of this frickin' guy."

Bolton unlatched his handgun from his holster. His eyes went wide when he saw the being. He had never seen anything like what he was witnessing, and Detective Andrew Bolton had seen a lot.

The tall being stood there dressed in an all-black robe. Its face was visible and covered in blood. Its hands were also drenched in the dark warm liquid, and it was ungodly tall.

Bolton froze in his tracks. He thought back to Karissa's words. At the time, he'd thought she was exaggerating. Not anymore. Her words, even in the most literal extent, could not prepare him for what the tall being's face looked like.

Shivers ran down his spine. *So cold.* It felt as if he were stranded in the Artic without even the clothes on his back.

The rest of the officers, about five in all, were pointing their handguns at the tall figure.

"Put your hands behind your head!" one officer commanded.

It didn't move; it just stood there with its artificial smile that seemed carved into its face and kept staring straight into the night.

"Put your goddamn hands over your head!" the officer repeated.

The tall creature then flew its arms up ninety degrees and held out its wrists. It caught all the officers by surprise, as every one of them flinched.

"All right, somebody cuff him!" another officer yelled.

Bolton, still frozen, stuttered, "W-wait, d-don't do it!" But he was too quiet, almost trancelike.

Another officer slowly walked up to the tall figure and pulled out his handcuffs. He still had his gun trained on the being.

"Wait, stop!" Bolton said loud enough so the police officer next to him could hear it.

"Wait, what?" said the officer.

Bolton snapped out of his trance. "DON'T DO IT!" he yelled.

The officer holding the cuffs looked over at Bolton. The tall being let out a loud, otherworldly roar and grabbed the officer by the jaw and put its other hand on his shoulder. With one pull, the top of the officer's head was ripped from the rest of his body. Blood went flying.

Bullets exited the barrels of police handguns immediately and rapidly. The tall being jumped to another officer, and the bullets might as well have been rubber, as it shook them off without worry.

It wasn't like the bullets didn't hurt it or penetrate its skin—they did. The being just didn't show it. It never made another sound other than its terrifying roar.

Then, it picked up another officer, grabbed him by the chest, and opened him up like a bag of potato chips. Guts dropped onto the pavement.

At that moment, Bolton fired a shot that hit the tall being in the side of its face, blowing what was left of its cheek and jaw off. It fell to the ground with a thud and died right there on the spot.

"God help us," said Bolton, as he scanned the ground in awe. The remaining officers just stood there too. Shocked beyond belief.

One of the officers broke the silence by screaming with rage. He walked up to the tall being and unloaded the rest of his handgun's clip into its torso. As the rest of the officers grabbed the one who couldn't contain his rage, Bolton took his radio in his hand.

"We need emergency services at Fremont Bridge," he said, while staring at the grotesque scene that lay before him. "Send everyone."

*

The next morning, a dense fog rolled through the city of Portland. The sunrise attempted to peek through the clouds but was unsuccessful. The Nelsons found themselves staying in a small hotel in the center of town.

Lewis was in the bathroom, taking a shower, while Karissa was lying in bed, holding onto a pillow while staring at the wall. Neither of them had gotten a wink of sleep.

When Lewis got out of the shower, he looked at himself in the mirror. He pushed his dark brown hair over to the left side. Then he put on some shaving cream and began to shave his beard off. Completely. He felt as if shaving the whole thing off would be like starting over in a way.

After shaving, he looked at his reflection. He knew he had to stay strong for Karissa. He never saw the tall man's face, but he could see how it had broken his wife down mentally. Plus, they both were heartbroken at the loss of Apollo. Lewis knew the only way he could help her was to move on and keep pushing forward.

He put on a red flannel and black jeans and walked out of the bathroom. Karissa was looking out the window now, still holding onto the pillow. Lewis walked up to her and wrapped his hands around her shoulders. He kissed the back of her head softly and said, "I love you, K."

She closed her eyes while leaking a tear. "I love you too."

Lewis kissed her head once more before walking over to his bag and pulling out his phone. "I'm going to take the day off, okay?"

She looked at him and said, "Me too."

Lewis then called up Jack Garcia and told him what had happened, and Karissa could hear Jack saying over the phone, "Yeah, buddy, you take a few days if you need to. Make sure she's okay."

Karissa stood up and walked to the window. When she looked outside, she saw a single police vehicle sitting idle in the parking lot by their door. Two police officers were inside.

The police vehicle reminded her of what she'd seen the night before. Then she thought of Apollo. She never saw the body of their beloved dog, but she didn't need to. She slowly moved toward her bag and pulled out some clothes.

Lewis, still on the phone, watched her make her way to the bathroom. He said his goodbyes to Jack and hung up the phone.

The shower turned on. Lewis sat there in silence and made sure Karissa was in the shower before turning on the hotel room TV. She was strong, always had been. But there were times when she would fall into an abyss. She had severe depression, and it would come and go at random times.

There were also those times—it had happened twice—where she would contemplate life and whether it was worth living. The doctor told Lewis to keep an eye on her, and make sure to stay with her during times when it seemed to be bad. Now, after the night before, he was on high alert.

It hadn't happened for a long time because the two of them had created such a strong bond that, no matter what sort of day they had, they could always come home and enjoy each other's company. They hardly fought, they were each other's best friend, and they could tell each other everything.

And Lewis knew that now, more than ever, she needed him. And he needed her.

He picked up the remote and attempted to switch through all the channels to find the news. He finally got to channel 7, the local news station, and in big text at the bottom of the screen it read, "Two Police Officers Killed in Standoff: Suspect Dead at the Scene."

Lewis had that same itch he had before. The itch that resided in the bottom of his brain.

The reporter on the screen said that a man had attempted to run from the police and then pulled a gun on them, causing a firefight that killed two police officers. They then went on to say that FBI Agent Andrew Bolton would address the issue for the public at around 8:00 a.m., which was about thirty minutes away. They then showed a drawing of a bald sixty-year-old man with blisters on his forehead and cheeks —the news anchor said that was the man involved in the shootout: "He stood around seven foot one."

Even though the man on TV had a pretty messed up face, Lewis knew it wasn't the face of the man from the night before. It wasn't a face that would traumatize his wife. She was a fighter.

Lewis was confused for a moment and began thinking of an explanation, but then he heard the water turn off in the bathroom.

"Lewis? Is everything okay?" Karissa asked softly. Her voice was shaking, Lewis could tell she had been crying in the shower.

He quickly turned the TV off and said, "Yeah, baby, every-thing's okay."

He needed to see what Bolton was going to say at the press conference, but he loved his wife more, and he knew she couldn't take any more of this. The best thing for her was to get her mind off of it.

She walked out of the bathroom with her hair still wet, wearing black leggings and a white T-shirt.

Lewis sat at the edge of the bed, He looked at her with his sad eyes, and she looked back at him. She could tell that he was trying his best to make her feel safe. She slowly walked up to him and sat down on his lap. They held each other, and she kissed him on the lips.

"What do we do?" she said while putting her head on his shoulder.

Lewis hesitated to speak before finally saying, "I don't know, baby...but whatever we do, we'll do it together. I promise."

She cracked a small smile. In her mind, they were going to love one another. The police were going to help. She knew it would be hard, but maybe she and Lewis could go back to their normal lives.

The thoughts that raced through Lewis' head were a bit different. That itch at the base of his skull, it got more irritating. All he could think of was that tall man. He felt like there was more to the story, and even though the police, and even the FBI, were on it, he felt as though he couldn't afford to wait that long.

## ~ 4 ~

A few weeks had passed. Karissa and Lewis had both gone back to work. They moved back into their house, and life just continued.

One night, Karissa woke to a panic attack, and Lewis talked her down.

He told her, "Whenever things are looking south, you got to find a way to keep going north." That saying stuck with the couple. When they told their therapist, Dr. Merlin stated that the saying should become a part of them. "Keep going north."

They would text each other at work to keep communication constant. Lewis was fulfilling his promise, his promise to keep Karissa going. Her mind had collapsed, and piece by piece, Lewis had to help rebuild it.

The city of Portland had put together a funeral for the police officers who were killed during the attack on Fremont Bridge. Andrew Bolton had spent the past few weeks in front of cameras and reporters. While Lewis' job was to help Karissa recover, Bolton had to worry about the whole city. Lewis had not talked to Detective Bolton since that night, but he had been busy.

As the days went on, Lewis kept thinking about his need for answers. And that itch in his brain got so persistent that it would wake him up at night. He would lie awake for hours, thinking about the tall man.

Where did he come from? What was his goal? Was he going to kill them that night? While going through these questions in his head, Lewis would get angry that he hadn't been the one to put the tall man down. He never brought up that feeling or the itch in his brain to anyone, not even Karissa, but he knew it was a problem and that it would continue.

*

A few days later, the Nelsons went over to the Garcias' home for dinner. It was a very nice home that sat on a hill with a nice view of Mount Hood. Both Lewis and Karissa were dressed nicely, and they'd brought a bottle of wine. As they pulled into the driveway, they noticed construction equipment outside of the garage.

Lewis remembered his wife telling him that the Garcias were adding onto their home—a new bedroom or something, he didn't remember that part. Although they were friends with the Garcias, the Nelsons weren't really into that whole fancy lifestyle. In fact, they never cared about tons of money, fancy clothes, or a big house. They never tried to prove anything to anyone. All that mattered to the Nelsons was to live together in happiness.

That was obviously not the case with the Garcias. Lisa, Jack's wife, was definitely the type of person who'd attend a ball or fundraiser every night of the week. And, although she was Karissa's best friend, she would drone on about the newest dresses or gossip about the city council, all things Karissa couldn't care less about.

Jack was Lewis' friend for sure, but they never really connected with each other on anything except sports. Often-times, Jack would let the power of his job go to his head. He had the kind of personality where he'd lift his head up high and talk down to employees, or even people at the grocery store.

There were a few instances where Lewis tried to tell Jack to knock it off, but Jack was Lewis' boss, so he had to play nice the majority of the time. Jack did, however, know how hard it had been for the Nelsons the past few weeks, so when he and his wife walked out and greeted them, it was all smiles and small talk.

The Garcias led the Nelsons into their home and began talking about the new addition on their house. After a few moments of chitchat about that, Karissa went into the kitchen to help Lisa finish up dinner, while the men went to grab a few beers from the fridge in the garage.

The conversations continued until dinner was ready, then they all proceeded to the dining room table and engaged in good food and laughter.

After everybody's bellies were full with the chicken and vegetables Lisa had prepared, it got a little quiet. Jack and Lewis were sitting in the living room, drinking their beer and watching the nightly football game, while Karissa and Lisa were in the kitchen, drinking wine and talking about each other's jobs.

At halftime, Jack got up and asked, "Want another beer, Lewis?"

Lewis casually replied, "Yeah, sure."

Jack walked to the kitchen while Lisa led Karissa up the stairs to show her where the new addition would be. Jack nonchalantly made sure the girls had made it up the stairs before returning to his seat. Jack handed Lewis his drink, to which he replied, "Thank you."

The sun had gone down now, and the sky was black and dark blue, with a small brushstroke of orange and purple directly above the horizon.

Jack looked around one more time and leaned into Lewis. He quietly said, "Hey, man." He stumbled a bit. "What—uh, how is Karissa doing? She holding up okay?"

Lewis could tell Jack wasn't comfortable asking the question. He sighed and said, "Yeah, I think so." His eyes were still glued to the halftime report. "She's getting through it."

"Well, if you guys need anything, you know we'll always be here for you," Jack said sincerely.

"Yeah, we really appreciate it, man. Really. Honestly," Lewis said while readjusting in his seat. "Socializing really seems to be helping her. I've been trying to keep her busy, you know? If she is just sitting on the couch at home, she'll have random anxiety attacks, but when we're out doing something, you know, dinner or hiking—hell, even just going for a drive, it helps clear her head."

Jack pressed his lips to the tip of his brown beer bottle and took a sip. "That's great, man," he said. "You know, Lisa has to go up to her parents' this weekend in Spokane; want me to see if Karissa can go?"

Lewis took a minute to think about it, then replied, "Yeah, I don't see why not. That might be nice to have some girl time."

At that moment, the girls began to walk down the stairs, both laughing about something. The game returned from its halftime break, and the two men's eyes instantly darted to the screen. They tapped their bottles together.

\*

After a week of work and therapy, the Nelsons were getting ready for Karissa's trip to Spokane. Lewis had a talk with their therapist, Dr. Merlin, to make sure Karissa was in the right state of mind for a trip. Dr. Merlin said as long as the communication keeps up and Karissa stays on top of her meds, she should be fine.

Lewis felt comfortable leaving his wife in the hands of Lisa Garcia and her parents, who lived in a very nice home on a lake near Spokane, Washington. It was going to be very peaceful, which was exactly what Lewis was hoping for.

While Karissa was spending her time packing and getting ready for the trip, Lewis continued with classes. He had a bigger plan set in place. Without Karissa there for the next three days, Lewis knew it was his chance to get to the bottom of what really went down at their home all those weeks ago.

Why had the tall man been at their house? Why did he not kill them? With Karissa around and her mind being as fragile as it was, he knew that this could be the only opportunity he would get.

They got the car all packed, and Lewis dropped Karissa off at the Garcias' house at around 9:00 a.m. on Friday morning. Jack was taking them to the airport, as Lewis had to make his 10:00 a.m. class. The girls wouldn't be back until Monday afternoon, which Lewis felt was a good thing.

He helped get his wife's suitcase out of his car, and then proceeded to put it in the back of Jack's. Before Karissa jumped into the Mercedes-Benz, Lewis pulled her aside.

"Hey, K. I just want to make sure, again, that you're okay with this."

She stared into his eyes and wrapped her arms around his neck. She kissed him passionately on the lips and said, "I love you," which answered his question.

She hopped in the back of the car and watched Jack and Lewis shake hands. Both men proceeded to get in their vehicles. Jack started his car and drove away as Lewis watched from the driver's seat of his Prius. His wife blew him a kiss, and he gave her a smile and a wave. Then he started up his windshield wipers and drove off.

*

At the University, Lewis parked in his reserved space. He sat there for a minute, as there was thirteen minutes before class started. He grabbed his bag and looked at the entrance of the psychology building. Students were flooding in. He recognized some of them, and they were no doubt heading to his class.

An itch arose at the stem of his spinal cord, where it met his skull.

"Damnit," he said while he threw his bag in the passenger seat and put his car in reverse. He peeled out of the parking lot and headed downtown, driving about fifteen miles over the speed limit. Sweat began to drip off his forehead.

He finally made his stop at the Portland Police Department. He got out of the car and frantically walked through the front doors. Lewis approached the officer at the counter and spoke quickly and loudly.

"I need to speak to Detective Bolton!"

The officer stared at him, unimpressed. "And what's your name?"

"Right now!" Lewis screamed.

The officer's eyes shot wide open, and he raised his hands, as if to calm Lewis down. "Okay, okay, give me a minute." The officer grabbed the phone next to him and dialed. "Someone's here to see Bolton."

Lewis heard chatter on the other end of the line. The officer said, "I don't know," then looked up at Lewis. "What's your name, kid?"

Lewis was caught off guard when the officer called him "kid"—the officer seemed only a few years older than he was.

However, when the officer called him "kid," the itch fizzled out, and Lewis began to calm down. He looked around as if he was confused by everything. It was surprising the officer didn't arrest him right there, as it looked like Lewis was on some sort of drug.

"Uh...Lewis, Lewis Nelson...sir."

The officer repeated the name into the phone. After he hung up, he told Lewis to sit down and someone would be with him soon.

The professor looked over at a small red chair in the corner of the station and went to sit. Before he could even touch his bottom to the chair, Bolton swung open the glass door behind the front desk.

"Mr. Nelson!" he said with a big smile.

Lewis greeted him back, and Bolton invited him to the back room. They headed to a small room that had a temporary nameplate on the door that read, "A. Bolton." The detective opened the door and asked Lewis to sit down. Then he walked behind his desk to his comfortable-looking black office chair. "So, what can I do you for?" asked Bolton.

Lewis took a moment to respond as he looked around the office. He noticed Bolton had framed pictures of people who were most likely his wife and two daughters.

"Nice office you got," Lewis said, still looking around.

"Oh, yeah, well, they gave me a temporary workspace until this case closes," Bolton replied.

"Is that your family?" Lewis asked, gesturing toward the pictures of the woman and two little girls.

"Yeah," Bolton said, adjusting in his seat. "My wife Donna and my two little ones, Jackie and Ruth. They're back home in Tennessee."

Lewis was obviously caught off guard by that. "Tennessee? Why're you working a case so far out west?"

"Well, I was stationed in Nashville but one night I got a call about this case in Portland, said I was specifically asked for."

"Huh," Lewis said. "Well, I'm not going to take any more of your time. I came in because, well, I need answers. I want to know why that man was at my house."

Bolton looked at the coffee mug that was sitting on his desk, then made eye contact with Lewis. "Well, Mr. Nelson—"

Lewis cut him off. "Lewis, please. I get called Mr. Nelson enough."

Bolton cleared his throat. "Right, Lewis. So I understand where you're coming from. I want to know too. That's why I'm still here and not back in Nashville."

"Right," Lewis said, understanding. "Well, can you tell me anything? Is there some kind of connection with me or Karissa? Or did I really lead him to my home from the night before?"

"Honestly, we don't know yet," said Bolton calmly. "The only thing I can tell you is that there were multiple sightings of this guy around the neighborhood, some dating back to a year ago. Every time it was called in, none of the guys here found anything. They started to think it was a joke or a hoax or something. Especially because nothing came of it. Nobody was harmed or went missing or anything of the sort."

"So, Detective Bolton—"

This time, the detective cut him off and gave a smirk. "Andrew."

"Andrew..." Lewis paused for a moment. "Nah, I'm going to stick with Bolton." The detective looked at him with a smile. "What do you, personally, think is going on?"

"Well, like I said, this guy was probably creeping around down in that neighborhood there for the past year. He was probably living in one of those abandoned buildings. There's some construction going on, and maybe it pissed him off, so he went out one night and took it out on someone. Maybe he liked doing it so much that he saw you there and, well, followed you back."

"You actually believe that? You saw his face too, right? That face traumatized my wife. I only got a glimpse, but I saw him well enough to know he was not human."

Bolton looked down at his mug again. "I will be honest; I've never seen anything like that before in my entire life. And you're right, he didn't seem human at all." He looked up from his mug and back at Lewis. "However, he's dead now, and I just have to check out a few more things before I close the case."

"So, you honestly think that was it? He's dead, end of story?"

Bolton replied, "Well, I'm going to check in with the coroner and see if I can learn anything more, but the police commissioner wants this whole thing to be over with. He lost good men, and he believes the best thing they can do is move on. I obviously have to check out a few more leads, but that seems to be the end of it. Especially 'cause the guy's dead."

"So, you don't think there is a bigger story here? Nothing seems off about this at all? Plus, who the hell was he? You haven't even given us a name yet."

"Honestly, Lewis, we don't know."

Lewis looked at Bolton with confusion, as well as some rage. "Wait, you guys still haven't identified him?"

"We can't," Bolton said, scratching his head. "Every test we've run has literally come back with nothing. This guy is nonexistent."

Lewis stood up from his chair. "Well, obviously the guy exists, and I want to know who the hell he his! How does this make any sense, Bolton?"

"Look, Lewis, I'm with you here," Bolton said, lowering his voice. "But even if I thought something was off, the bureau won't listen unless the rest of the police department backs my story up. Meaning I would have to find something compelling that would keep the case open, and I'm just not finding anything. There's no evidence of anything more."

Lewis began to shout. "Don't have the evidence yet?! How about my wife being traumatized?! She won't ever be the same again, do you understand that? How about the bastard killing my dog? How about the two officers who died on that bridge?! You were there, Bolton! You saw him! There's evidence all over the place!"

Bolton tried to calm him, but it was too late. Lewis turned around and walked out of Bolton's office, slamming the door behind him.

"Damnit," he mumbled under his breath. He was upset for sure, because deep down he knew something was off. He shook his head and began to replay everything in his mind. His eyes panned around the room until they met the photo of his family that was facing him on his desk. He proceeded to pull out his cell phone and call his wife.

Bolton felt instant relaxation when his wife said, "Hey, honey!"

He started glowing. "Hey, baby, how are you? How are the girls?"

"They're good. I just picked Jackie up from school for her dentist appointment. And the Johnsons invited the girls and I over for dinner tonight, so we might go and do that later."

"Oh, that'll be fun," Bolton said while adjusting his watch.

"How's everything going there?" Donna asked pleasantly.

"It's...uh..." Bolton looked at a group of police officers that had just entered the building. They were all laughing at one another. Bolton refocused. "It's crazy. The department wants us to close the case, but there's a part of me that feels like I can do something more."

"What are you going to do?" she asked.

"Well, the bureau asked me to stay a few weeks to make sure this thing is closed completely. There are a few things that I still have to look into, but nothing major."

"Be careful, Andy," Donna said, sounding very concerned.

"When am I not careful?" Bolton said, chuckling.

"I'm serious," Donna said. "The girls and I, we need you."

"Baby," Bolton said, understanding her concern. "I promise I'm coming home soon, okay?"

They said their goodbyes as Bolton hung up the phone. He sat there and thought about what Lewis said. He reached into his drawer and pulled out a manila folder. Inside were the photos of the crime scene. One photo showed one of the dead officers with his jaw lying two feet away from his body. He was lying in a pool of blood.

Another picture showed the other officer lying on his back. There was nothing between his upper torso and his waist except his innards. The next photo made chills roll down Bolton's spine to the point where he shook like he was cold. It was a close-up of the tall man's face. He still didn't know the man's name or where he came from. He was a ghost and a complete mystery.

However, that face. It would haunt Bolton forever, and he cringed as he examined it. In the photo, the man's eyes were wide open. Well, he didn't have eyelids. One side of his cheek and jaw was a mangled mess from were Bolton shot and killed him. The other side was still cut into a permanent smile.

Bolton then looked at the drawing they'd showed on the news. He knew that the department couldn't allow a face like that to be shown on TV, so the commissioner of the Portland Police Department, John Byrd, had them draw a face. They had to give the media something.

Bolton sent the photos to the FBI, and in response they had told him to wait and make sure everything was one hundred percent wrapped up. He knew why Lewis was so angry though. Commissioner Byrd's response to the whole thing was to forget and move on. He believed that as long as the man was dead, it would be best for the city to just keep going forward.

A moment later, the phone rang. Bolton answered it quickly. It was the coroner.

*

Lewis was angry. Angrier than he had been in a long time. He drove back to his house, cursing every second. He got to his driveway and halted his car aggressively. Then he screamed and punched his steering wheel.

It felt good.

He did it again. He cursed loudly and punched again and again and again until he got it out of his system. He wasn't sure why he was so angry. The man who had stalked his family and killed his dog was dead. Was it the fact that the police knew nothing? What was keeping him up at night? What was that annoying itch he felt at the base of his skull?

He looked down at his phone and saw he had three missed calls from Jack Garcia. There was a voicemail too. Lewis touched the screen and put the phone up to his ear. A bead of sweat rolled down his forehead as he looked at himself in the rearview mirror and noticed his face was a bright shade of red. He rolled his fingers through his hair as he listened to the voicemail.

"Lewis, I dropped off Karissa and Lisa and came back to sit in on your class, only to find that you didn't show up. What's going on, man?"

Lewis sighed and dropped his head. He continued to listen.

"You have to tell me if you're going to miss class, okay? I have no problem with finding someone else to step in and help you out, but I need to know. Call me back."

Lewis lowered the phone and clicked the button that locked the screen. He grabbed his bag from the seat next to him and swung it over his shoulder as he got out of the car.

He felt the cold mist on his face, and he walked inside his house. It felt good. Cooling.

He threw his bag on the couch and looked around. The memories of that night flooded his head. He walked into his and Karissa's bedroom and looked at his bedside window. And, although it was no longer there, he could still see the bloody handprint the tall man had left as he stalked them.

Watching.

Waiting.

For what?

Lewis scanned the room and noticed Apollo's food bowl. It was ceramic and decorated with stars and planets. He remembered when Karissa had brought that home from a pottery class she took in college. She'd left it on the counter with a box of dog treats that she'd tied with a bow. Apollo was just a puppy then.

Lewis let out a sigh and closed his eyes. It was a happy memory. Unfortunately, it was followed by a sad realization.

He walked into the bathroom and undressed then proceeded to turn the shower on. More memories kept flooding his mind. He remembered meeting Karissa for the first time.

Lewis was never into drinking or partying, but he loved football. He knew the game inside and out, but he liked the strategy part more than the hitting. That's why he never played.

But on one rainy night in Eugene, the Ducks were playing the Beavers in their classic rivalry game. His best friend at the time, Jacob, was holding a watch party for the game at his apartment. Chips and wings were laid out across the table, and all sorts of alcohol was sitting on the counter for people to enjoy.

About fifteen people made it to the apartment by the time the game started. Lewis was drinking an iced tea while everyone else was drinking alcohol. Halfway through the first quarter, they heard a knock at the door. Jacob yelled, "I'll get it!" as he shot up from his seat and jumped to answer. He opened the door and greeted a small group of four girls. One of the girls hugged Jacob and introduced him to the other three.

Lewis' eyes were still glued to the screen as Jacob walked over and said, "Hey, guys, this is Janelle, Kelsey, Audrey, and..." He leaned over and asked the smaller girl in the back, "What was your name? I'm sorry."

She said it softly.

"Karissa," Jacob said.

Lewis turned his head. He liked that name. When he saw her, it was like he got hit by a train. She had her shoulder-length brown hair in curls, and she was wearing big thick glasses. She was thin and wearing a denim jacket over a white T-shirt. She had on black leggings and white converse.

Their eyes met.

She could clearly see he was glowing at the sight of her, but she didn't know what to do at first. She looked away but kept finding herself meeting his gaze. She blushed and gave him a smirk.

Jacob was introducing all of the people who were already at the party, and as he introduced Lewis, everybody said hi.

However, Lewis replied, "Hi, everyone," while keeping his eyes on Karissa.

Jacob invited everyone to eat, drink, and have fun watching the game. He made a little joke about how Ducks eat Beavers or something, but Lewis didn't care.

He got up from the couch and walked over to Karissa, who was now in the kitchen with her friends, deciding what beer to drink. She looked up and saw him coming her way. Audrey saw it too and nudged Karissa's arm and laughed.

"Hey, Karissa, right?" Lewis said with a big, charming smile.

"Yeah, you're Lewis?" she asked while blushing.

"Lewis Nelson. At your service," he said, thinking he was being classy by taking a small bow. He regretted that decision when Karissa's friends started laughing.

She chuckled and asked, "So, you go to school here?"

"Yup, I'm mastering in psychology. I want to be a teacher. What about you?"

"Wow, a psychology teacher, huh? That's pretty sexy," she said laughing. "I'm majoring in journalism. I'm a senior."

"Well, it's very nice to meet you, Karissaaaa..." He drug out her name waiting for her to finish the sentence.

"Brown," she said. "And you too, Mr. Nelson." She smirked.

That lit a fire in Lewis he had never felt before.

"So, what's good here?" Karissa asked while gesturing toward the alcohol.

Lewis looked down at his cup. "Uh...I actually don't really know," he said, chuckling nervously. She looked a little confused. He raised his cup. "Sweet tea," he said, laughing.

Karissa's friend group laughed again. But this time it wasn't at Lewis, even though that's what he thought. Janelle looked at Karissa and smiled at her.

"Do you have another tea?" Karissa asked, blushing. Lewis realized she didn't really drink either. He gave her a big smile and said, "I sure do."

They spent the rest of the night watching the game and laughing. When Karissa's friends got too drunk toward the end of the fourth quarter, she told Lewis she had to take them home and look after them. He didn't want the night to end.

She noticed and said, "I really want to see you again."

His frown turned into a huge glowing smile. "Can I have your phone number?" he asked.

"Of course!" she said, smiling back.

As she left, Lewis watched her walk to her car with her three friends, all very drunk. She looked back at him and smiled. He smiled and waved as he watched her pull out of the parking lot.

"Holy shit," he said happily.

Lewis stepped out of the shower with a big smile on his face. Remembering those times always made him happy. He remembered their wedding too. It was outside, and a storm came out of nowhere and flooded the whole thing.

He and Karissa just laughed even though they were both soaking wet. The more he thought about these memories, the happier he was. He grabbed his phone and texted Karissa.

*I love you, K. Have a safe flight. Keep going north.*

He looked at himself in the mirror. Then, out of nowhere, he felt an itch where his spine and skull met. The happiness turned into rage. Somebody had come to his house and traumatized the love of his life. He wanted to know why. He needed to know why.

"FUCK!" he screamed as he punched the mirror into shards of glass.

*

Bolton walked into a white room that was lit up by florescent lights. A man in a white jacket was sitting in front of a table with a body on it. Bolton noticed that the body's feet were hanging off the table as he greeted the man.

"Mark," he said while shaking the man's hand. "I'm Detective Bolton with the FBI."

"Nice to meet you Detective Bolton," Mark said. "I've got something for you to see." He gestured to the body on the table, then walked over to his desk, pulled out two blue latex gloves, and put them on.

"So, this is our guy, huh?" Bolton said, staring at the sheet that covered the body.

"Yes. So, it obviously took us a while to examine, but we've never had a person in here like this before." Mark folded the sheet down to show the face.

"Jesus Christ," Bolton said.

"Yeah, not very handsome, I can tell you that much. But look, his eyelids were burnt off. You can tell by the black soot around them. How this man could see at all is beyond me since the burning of the eyelids seems to have happened a long time ago. If we move down to the mouth, you can see it's carved from the corner of his mouth back toward the molars. If we move further down, we can see some rotting here on the neck. But here's the thing that I need to show you." Mark folded the sheet down further to the waist where the man's torso was showing.

"What the hell?" Bolton said slowly, his eyes widening. The tall man had large scars all around his body. There were three holes where the bullets from the police officers had entered on the bridge. But the thing that caught Bolton's eye was a large scar in the shape of a spiral on the man's chest. It was different than all of the other scars. This one hadn't healed properly. It was red and bulging, as if the smallest cut into it would release a pool of blood.

"I didn't want to disturb this by cutting through it until someone saw it," Mark said to Bolton while he was examining the spiral. "Does this symbol mean anything to you?"

Bolton, refusing to take his eyes off of the spiral, said, "This thing might be deeper than we thought."

*

"What do you mean? The case is closed, Bolton," Commissioner Byrd said, "He was a crazy person—of course he could've just done this to himself."

"No way," Bolton said confidently. "Look at these pictures. There are scars all over his body. Mark said he could tell the spiral on his sternum was done by somebody else by how it healed and how perfect the shape was."

"Bolton, I get that you are FBI, but you need to listen here. This case is closed, and that's it. This guy was obviously unstable and—"

"You honestly think this case is closed? Are you kidding me? I didn't buy that shit even before the autopsy. Lewis Nelson didn't buy that shit, and he's a goddamn teacher! Don't be a fucking idiot—"

Byrd cut him off. "Hey! Look, you may be a fed, but this is still my department, you understand me? And this department is saying the case is closed."

"I'm sure those officers who died on the bridge would say different. I'm calling this in." Bolton looked at Byrd with anger and pulled out his phone as he stormed out of the office.

\*

"Ask Nelson if he's ever seen that spiral before. He might have a connection to it somehow," said Agent Phil over the phone. He was one of Bolton's close friends in the FBI.

"Look, I understand that if Byrd doesn't keep the case going, you can't send backup, and I have to go home. But can you send anything? Anybody?" Bolton asked.

"No. Bolton, you are going to have to do this alone. We're keeping you there for just a couple more weeks so you can wrap this up. Boss wants you back soon."

"Understood," Bolton said while sighing.

"I'll make a couple calls and see if anybody knows anything about that symbol. I'll keep you updated," Agent Phil said before hanging up.

Bolton shook his head in disappointment.

\*

The sun was going down, and Lewis was watching TV. He was in the basement because he was not comfortable sleeping in his bedroom without Karissa there, and without Apollo, the whole house felt lonely.

He had wrapped his hand in a bandage to help stop the bleeding from when he punched the mirror, and he had a sweet tea in the other hand. The sound of heavy rain began to pound on his window.

He turned the TV up a little louder, but then he heard his phone rang. He figured it was Jack, who he still hadn't called back. After it stopped ringing, it rang again. And again. Lewis grabbed the phone and cursed. Without looking at who it was, he turned it on silent and put the phone back down.

After about five minutes, there was a knock on the front door.

"Damn it."

He paused the TV and grunted as he got up. He walked to the door and opened it. There stood Detective Andrew Bolton, wearing a black trench coat and holding a briefcase.

"Lewis, can we talk?"

"Yeah, come on in." Lewis sighed while opening the door wider, allowing Bolton to enter.

"There's something I want to show you," Bolton said while following Lewis through the house. "Mrs. Nelson home?"

"No, she's in Spokane with a friend," Lewis said as he walked to the fridge and pointed at the dinner table to silently tell Bolton to sit down. "I have beer, tea, milk, and orange juice."

Bolton looked at Lewis' hand and said, "Uh...I'll have a beer, thanks."

Lewis mumbled to himself, "Beer it is." He grabbed two bottles and walked to the table. He handed one to Bolton.

"You got a bottle opener, Lewis?" Bolton asked politely.

"It's a twist off," Lewis said, annoyed. He didn't care for Detective Bolton at the moment because of what happened earlier that day, and he wanted Bolton to know it.

"What happened to your hand? If you don't mind me asking," Bolton said.

"I actually do mind, thank you," Lewis said with a fake smile. "Why are you here, Bolton?"

"I spoke with the coroner today. I need to ask you a few things." Bolton took something out of his briefcase. "The man is still unidentifiable. However, there is one thing that we discovered on his torso. Can you take a look at this symbol and tell me if it means anything to you?"

Bolton slid the photo of the spiral carved into the tall man's chest across the table. Lewis' face cringed as he examined it.

"What the hell is this?" Lewis asked with his eyes still glued to the photo.

Bolton cleared his throat. "Well, we are unaware of any kind of relation to that symbol. The red, bulging scars that make it up are strange. It's precise. I believe—"

Lewis cut him off. "Somebody else did it to him."

"Exactly," Bolton said smirking.

"Well, symbols like these can be used in cults and things of that nature. I mean, that's where my mind goes when I look at this."

Bolton cut in. "That's what I was thinking."

Lewis continued, "Usually, when we see symbols used by cultists they are demonic symbols like pentagrams, or even hieroglyphics from Egyptian mythology. I've never seen anything like this before. I mean, it obviously isn't any kind of cult I've ever heard of before."

"And unfortunately," Bolton said, "it seems to be a violent cult."

"No shit," Lewis said, looking at Bolton. All the irritation and annoyance Lewis had felt simply faded. He knew he was right. There was something more to this story, and that's all that mattered to him.

"But cults typically follow a supernatural being or scenario," Lewis continued. "That's why they use these symbols. They want to befriend the supernatural entity that they worship. They wish to honor it. So, the question is, what kind of religion or supernatural entity uses a spiral?"

Intrigued, Bolton looked at Lewis and said, "I don't know. Figuring that out is my next step though."

"What did your fed buddies say about this?" Lewis asked, glancing up at Bolton

"I'm having somebody look into this symbol, but other than that, I'm on my own."

"I'm going to help you."

"No," Bolton said, standing up. "I came here to ask you about the symbol, not to recruit you into this investigation."

"Okay, so you're opening the case up again, right? Because it sure as hell isn't closed."

Bolton let out a sigh. "No, actually. Byrd wants the city to forget and move on."

"Still? Are you serious?" Lewis raised his eyebrows. "What about the FBI? They can't just let something like this go, right?"

"The FBI won't send more backup unless Byrd wants it. Especially since he closed the case and the suspect is deceased."

Lewis looked at Bolton in the eyes. "So, what you're saying is, you're alone."

Bolton nodded.

"Okay. I'm helping you investigate."

"I can't allow that. I'm sorry," the detective said.

Lewis looked at Bolton with an electrifying glance. "Bolton, let me ask you something. Why did you become an FBI agent? What drove you to this profession?"

Bolton sat back down with a small sigh and took his eyes away from Lewis.

"I grew up in a really small town, 'bout thirty miles outside of Billings. You know, Montana. My dad was a preacher. My mom stayed at home and looked after us. Well, we had this family in town, the Currys. They were the only family in town who never showed up to Sunday service, most likely because they were too busy smoking crack and doing lines of cocaine. And our town was tiny. I mean, if you were walking through on Sunday morning, you wouldn't see a single soul because everybody was at church. Well, everyone but the Currys."

He paused to take a sip of his beer.

"One Sunday, the daughter went missing. Nobody knew where she went. The Currys knew where everybody would be, so they drove to the church and barged through the door mid-service. There was about six of them, and they were all holding guns. They demanded that whoever took their little girl give her up and nobody would get hurt. Well, the sheriff stood up and tried to calm Mr. Curry down, but it wasn't working. Curry grabbed an old lady and punched her with the butt of his gun. Sheriff went for his gun, and Currys started shooting up the place. One of them aimed his gun at me, and my dad ran in front of the bullet. Both of my parents were killed that day. If it wasn't for the other officers in the church, the Currys might've killed the entire town. Five members of the family were killed, but Mr. Curry escaped. I spent the entire summer trying to find him. When I did, I put a bullet in his head. Funny thing is, the daughter ran away with a boyfriend and just didn't tell anybody. So, when I turned eighteen, I became a cop. Wanted to look out for the town and make sure nothing like that happened again. I lost everything that day."

He finished the last of his beer then continued, "A few years down the road, there were some murders down by Yellowstone, and they called all of us there. I was the one to find the guy, and when I did, I was invited to join the FBI. So, I went to the academy and got stationed in Nashville. Got a call about a murder in Portland, and here we are."

Lewis stood up and looked at him intensely. "Bolton," he said, speaking slowly, "I may not be a cop or an FBI agent, but I am a psychology professor. I study things like this, and you don't have anybody else in your corner except me. So, I'm helping you."

Bolton looked down and sighed.

"Shit," he mumbled.

## ~ 5 ~

Lewis awoke in his bed on a crisp Saturday morning. He'd gotten the best sleep he had in a while. Rain tapped on the windows as he flipped his body to get out of bed. He slipped on his tan moccasins and walked into the kitchen. After a brief stretch, he started making himself a pot of coffee while he opened the fridge and pulled out a carton of eggs, milk, butter, diced onions, and cheese. He turned the stove on and began his omelet.

The phone rang.

"Hello?" Lewis answered giddily.

"Good morning, Lewy!" said Karissa spritely.

"Good morning to you too, baby. How's Spokane?" he asked while whisking the eggs.

"It's good. Lisa's parents are super nice. We spent the day playing board games. I mean, they live on the lake, but it just won't stop raining."

"Yeah, same here. I don't think it's going to stop anytime soon."

"What about you? What've you been up to?" she asked happily.

"Nothing really. Just hanging out, making omelets." He poured the whisked eggs into the pan, making a loud sizzling sound.

"Oh, god, I am so jealous right now. I love your omelets," she said. Lewis could practically hear her mouth watering.

"I'll make you one when you get home, don't worry," Lewis said, chuckling.

"You better! How was work yesterday?"

Lewis stopped chuckling immediately. "Uh, good. It was good."

"Everything okay?" she asked, as she could easily tell that question had caught him off guard.

"Okay, I'll be honest with you, I didn't go."

"What? Why not?" she asked, shocked.

"After you left, I got a bad stomachache. Been sick all night."

"Yeah, that's why you're cooking an omelet right now, right?" she said, unimpressed with his lie.

"How is it I'm a college professor, but when I talk to you, I turn back into a twelve-year-old?" he said, laughing.

"Lewis, really." She was not interested in his jokes at the moment. "What is going on? Are you okay?"

"Yes, K. I am fine." He spoke slowly. "I just didn't feel like myself. But I'm all good now. I promise."

"Are you sure? I can come back if—"

"No, no!" he said, cutting her off. "Don't worry about me, I really feel a whole lot better, and I'll be back to work on Monday. Just enjoy your weekend, okay? Tell Lisa I said hi."

"Okay. Let me know if you need anything, alright, baby?" she said, a little worried. "I love you."

"I love you too," he said before hanging up the phone. He grabbed the skillet and flipped the omelet.

*

Lewis got out of the shower and wrapped a towel around his waist, then headed to his closet where he picked out some black jeans, black boots, a gray T-shirt, and a brown leather jacket. He styled his hair in its typical wave, using his phone as a mirror for obvious reasons. After he was dressed, Lewis picked up his cell phone and called Detective Bolton.

"Yeah, hello?" Bolton said, a little rushed.

"What's going on, man, you alright?" Lewis asked concerned.

"Yeah, just these damn cops here. Not one of them gives a shit about this."

"Well, that's why I am here," Lewis said confidently.

"I still don't like this, Lewis. I'm perfectly capable of handling this on my own," Bolton said while walking into the men's room.

"Can't back out now, man. With my help, we are going to figure this out and understand why Mr. Tall Asshole was targeting my family, and also why he had a giant spiral carved onto his fucking sternum."

"You know, for a psychology professor, you're pretty vulgar."

"You know, for an FBI agent, you sure look like a pretty boy."

"Okay, I'll give you that one," Bolton said while looking at himself in the mirror and chuckling. "Meet me at the corner where Hopkins was killed. I'm going to do a search around that area to see if I can find anything else."

"Okay, I'm out the door."

"Wait, Lew—"

But Lewis had hung up.

"Why do I feel like this guy's going to be the death of me?" Bolton said to himself in the mirror.

*

When Bolton arrived at the corner of Thirteenth and Grand Hill, he saw Lewis' car already parked on the side of the road. Bolton parked his SUV right behind it, but there was no sign of Lewis.

When Bolton got out of his car, he adjusted his shoulder holster beneath his black trench coat. It was another foggy day in the city and the crisp, cold air flowed through Bolton's hair. He walked to the sidewalk, where he noticed plenty of flowers and pictures of Patrick Hopkins, along with a few candles that had been drowned in the rain.

The detective decided to walk around the block and see if he could find Lewis. He looked down an alleyway but the fog from the rain was so dense he could only see a faded green neon sign toward the end of the alley. He went back to the corner and looked up at the streetlights. It was about 11:00 a.m., but the lights were still on due to the fog.

Bolton kept following the streetlights until he saw the silhouette of a person getting closer and closer with every step he took. He eventually realized it was Lewis. But he was just standing there, staring at a building off to the right.

"Lewis, you alright?" Bolton asked, but Lewis just kept his eyes on the building.

"If our guy is part of a cult, I think he might be living here, don't you? An abandoned chapel in the middle of downtown Portland?"

"What the hell?" Bolton turned and looked at the broken building. "I honestly had no idea this was here."

"Of course you didn't, Kentucky boy," Lewis joked. "You just got here."

"Tennessee, but that's okay."

"This place has been around for a long time. Nobody thinks anything of it other than the scary stories kids tell each other on Halloween. Anyway." He put his hand on the detective's shoulder. "Let's do it," Lewis said while walking up to the chapel.

"Wait, we can't go into just any building."

"It's abandoned, so..."

"Still, there are laws against it."

Lewis looked at him in disappointment. "Jesus Christ, aren't you an FBI agent?"

"Fine," Bolton said, putting his hands in his pockets as he followed Lewis up to the chapel.

While Bolton truly thought there was more to this case, he was still hesitant about allowing a civilian to investigate alongside him. And seeing Lewis act like a completely different guy than he had been the day before didn't sit right with him, but he was here and he decided to go along with it.

"Move," Bolton commanded as they got to the door.

"What?" Lewis asked, surprised by the tone of Bolton's voice.

"I'm going to kick the door down."

Lewis raised his eyebrows and said, "Be my guest." He stepped aside.

Bolton pulled out his gun, pointed it at the door, then hit the door hard with his foot. The door slammed onto the floor, making a loud bang. The smell of death and disease proceeded to hit both men's nostrils like a truck.

"Oh, shit," Lewis said while putting his arm over his nose. "Bolton, something's dead in there, man."

The detective nodded in confirmation and held his gun up higher. He was very focused and almost unfazed by the smell. He began to walk inside. Lewis tried to follow but got another whiff of the foul smell, turned back around, and gagged. It was too dark to see inside, so Bolton pulled out a small flashlight and held it up by his gun. The inside of the church was rotting and full of flies and stains of all different colors. Lewis, after holding down his breakfast, walked inside with his shirt pulled over his nose. Bolton shined his light in one corner of the front room. There was a large orange and black stain.

"What the hell is that?" Lewis said, disgusted.

"Most likely vomit, piss, or shit. Or all of the above," Bolton said with a straight face.

Lewis turned around to gag again.

"Hey," Bolton said seriously. "Either go outside and yak or keep it together and shut up."

"You got it," Lewis said, swallowing his breakfast for a second time.

Bolton kept his gun high. He began to walk through a doorway, which led to the nave. As he walked in, it got darker and darker. Lewis followed closely behind.

As Bolton shined his light on the pews, he noticed three objects sitting in the front row toward the altar.

"Psst," Bolton whispered to Lewis. He shined the light directly on them, and it looked as though there were three people sitting with white sheets over their heads.

Bolton leaned closer to Lewis. "They're definitely bodies," he whispered.

Bolton walked closer. Slowly, very slowly. One of his footsteps caused a loud creak in the floorboards.

Lewis stopped him in his tracks.

"What is it?" Bolton asked.

"Look at the sheets. They're white."

"So?"

"Nothing else in here is," he whispered.

Bolton understood. The church was unbelievably dirty, but the sheets that lay on the three bodies were extremely white and clean. Somebody had been there recently, and it definitely wasn't the tall man.

Bolton reached over to his radio. "This is Detective Bolton; I need backup down here at 1351 Grand Hill Road," he said quietly into the radio.

"Copy that, Bolton." The voice that replied was loud.

"Shit!" Lewis whispered loudly.

Bolton kept his gun aimed at the three bodies under the sheets and began to walk toward them.

"What the hell are you doing?" Lewis quietly asked.

The detective continued walking. "Go back outside," he whispered to Lewis without taking his eyes off the three figures.

"What? I'm not going to—"

"Get the HELL back outside," Bolton hissed.

"No!"

Lewis stayed right where he was.

As Bolton realized how stubborn Lewis actually was, he arrived at the front of the pews. He found himself within reaching distance of the bodies under the sheets. He put his flashlight in his mouth, reached out to grab one of the sheets, and pulled it off quickly. It revealed a skinny, almost mummified person. Their jaw was nowhere to be seen, and their brown, rotting skin was loosely attached to the bones of the body. The eyes were hollowed out holes, and the body's nose was missing, along with the ears. There was a cardboard sign hanging around the neck. On it was the name, "Clarence."

"Jesus Christ," Lewis said, shocked.

Bolton, still looking at the body, moved to the next one, grabbed the sheet, and pulled it off. This time, it was a mannequin. Well, it had the torso, arms, and head of a mannequin. Its legs were missing. The mannequin's eyes were both painted on with an almond shape and then two small dots. The mouth was smeared in a dark red substance that had dried down to the mannequin's private area, in which a hole was carved.

And carved right above the hole was the name, "Barbara."

Lewis and Bolton looked at each other in fear and disgust. After an unspoken agreement that what they were seeing was unbelievable, Bolton moved to the third and final sheet.

He let out a sigh and pulled it off with a quick tug. A large, skinny man in a black robe sat there. He had no eyelids nor lips, and a permanent smile was carved into his face. Both Lewis and Bolton jumped at the sight of this.

It looked just like the tall man on the bridge.

Bolton lightly tapped the person's head with the tip of his handgun. No movement.

"Wait, what the hell?" Bolton said while squinting and looking more closely. He noticed a small, carved spiral right in between the lifeless eyes.

As he got closer to examine it, the lifeless being shot up as fast as a bullet, shoving Bolton with so much force that he flew back and collided with the altar, breaking it into pieces.

The being stood up and let out a loud, inhuman scream.

"Bolton!" Lewis yelled before turning toward the being. He could barely see, as Bolton's flashlight had fallen out of his mouth when he hit the altar. Now it offered no help, as it faced the opposite direction. The scream was so loud it rang in Lewis' head. He felt an itch at the base of his skull. The evil being then jumped onto Lewis and pinned him down. Its giant, lifeless eyeballs stared right into Lewis'. Then it quieted down and moved its face close to Lewis. It began to drool and the professor turned his head in disgust. The being let out a loud, otherworldly groan.

Bolton awoke and noticed what was happening. He picked up his pistol, which lay next to him, and aimed it in the general direction of the groan. Bolton couldn't see though, because of the dark, so he looked around quickly and saw his flashlight. He jumped to it, grabbed it with one hand, and aimed it at Lewis and the being. Now that he was able to see, he aimed his gun, but before he could shoot, blood rushed into his eyes and blinded him.

"Fuck!" Bolton screamed, attempting to wipe the blood away.

"Bolton! Shoot him!" Lewis yelled, still facing away from the being.

The being roared, and its mouth opened so wide, Lewis could see everything inside it.

Bolton screamed and shot three times, still unsure of his vision.

The sound of a bullet tearing through brains echoed in the room. The being fell on top of Lewis.

Both men sat there in silence, breathing heavily.

*

The rain continued to pour, and a thick layer of fog still had its hands all over downtown. Red and blue lights flashed, and yellow crime tape was strewn about the abandoned chapel, extending all the way out to the middle of the street. Three police officers in bright neon yellow vests were directing traffic. It was a crime scene.

Both Bolton and Lewis were sitting down with coffee cups and blankets that the other officers had given them. The professor was staring off into the distance, lost in thought.

The detective noticed, so he got up and walked over to him and asked if he was okay.

Lewis never said anything. He was so lost in the events that had just occurred. After Bolton's call for backup, an ambulance and two police cars arrived seven minutes later. When the police entered the chapel, all they heard were the short and quick breaths of the two men, who were frozen in shock.

"I'm sorry I got you involved in this, man," Bolton said, letting out a sigh. "I should've never let this happen."

Lewis turned his head slowly and looked Bolton in the eyes. "If it wasn't for me, you never would've found this place. I did this, Bolton. Not you. Not the police department. Me. A college professor. I just opened the case back up for you. I gave you the best evidence you could have. Easily." He spoke in a very chilling and lifeless tone.

Bolton, although upset by Lewis' words, knew he was right. He had no help from the Portland Police Department and no help from the FBI. The only person who gave a damn about him was this cocky-but-smart psychology professor. Lewis took a sip of his coffee as he scoffed.

"You're right," Bolton admitted. "I wouldn't have been able to do any of this without you. You helped me finish this case."

"Are you serious?" Lewis turned his head quickly, causing beads of rain that had collected on his hair to fly. "This case isn't nearly closed. This case is just beginning. We don't know shit about these people—this *cult*, I should say, as it clearly is, and I intend to figure this out."

Bolton tried to cut in, but Lewis didn't let him.

"What is their main reason for being here?" Lewis continued. "Who is the leader of the cult? Where are the rest of them? Both of these people were tall and had grotesque faces. They were both in black robes, right? In a typical cult, the followers all wear the same sort of outfit and have the same markings. The leader has a different look than the rest of them and can usually stand out. Since both of the beings we've seen here were wearing the same stuff, I highly doubt they are in charge."

He took a sip of his coffee before continuing. "Look at Heaven's Gate. That cult wore matching clothes and eventually killed themselves because they thought it was going to allow them to board a UFO that followed a comet. There's always an endgame. I want to know why these people were here in this church and why they both have these slashed-up faces."

"I honestly wish this was a Heaven's Gate situation. They could've just killed themselves, and this nightmare would've been over. But I agree. This group, or cult, whatever they are, they obviously have violent intentions," Bolton said, running his hand through his waterlogged hair.

Lewis leaned closer to Bolton and whispered, "I also think we need to get a good look at this evidence. I just don't have a very good feeling. A mummified body and a disgusting mannequin? What the hell are those for?"

The two men shook their heads in disbelief at the memory of what they saw.

"At least now Byrd will finally listen and allow more feds to come here and help, right?" Lewis asked.

"Yeah, he has no choice now. I'll get him to do a search in the nearby buildings to see if there's anything else like this here. My buddy at the bureau is doing research to see if this symbol belongs to anybody."

"Okay. I'm going to go to the library tonight and do a little research of my own. Let me know if they find anything worth mentioning." Lewis got up.

"Oh, Lewis," Bolton started, "are there any more local myths or legends I should know about?"

Lewis took a minute to think. "Not unless you count the boogeyman," he said, laughing

"I do, actually," Bolton said under his breath.

As Lewis was walking away, Bolton knew that he was a part of this investigation now. He felt as though he had to be. It was just a feeling. An itch at the base of his skull.

*

On that cool and crisp Saturday morning, Karissa had just gotten off the phone with Lewis. She looked out the window and sighed as the rain tapped it.

Lisa Garcia walked into the living room and saw Karissa's sadness, as she wasn't hiding it very well.

"Hey, are you okay?" she asked, stopping in her tracks.

"Lewis didn't go to work yesterday," Karissa said, looking down. "He didn't give me a reason either."

"Honey, I promise you he's not with another girl; that boy couldn't survive without you."

"What? No." Karissa said, raising her eyebrows and turning her head toward Lisa. "I'm afraid that me leaving might've been a bad idea. He's all alone now and...I don't know. I just hope he's okay."

"I'm sure he's fine. I'll talk to Jack today and see if he can take Lewis out for a beer or something," Lisa said with kind eyes. Karissa said thank you, and they hugged each other.

"My parents said they want to go to an antique store later, so that'll be fun." Lisa smiled, hoping Karissa would be excited, as she could tell Karissa was having a hard time. Plus, the whole mood was sad, as the rain just wouldn't stop.

On the bright side, she was so tired of being inside that when Lisa said they were going out to do something, she was excited, which pleased Lisa.

"I just have to write to Jerry today. He told me I can write a little story on Spokane's culture and how it compares to Portland's," Karissa said, somewhat annoyed.

"He's still giving you small stories?"

"Well, no. Actually, my last one was pretty big, and it was very well-received. He's just giving me time to get my shit together again before I get another story like that. Or at least, that's what I'm hoping. He's not the most open guy in the world," she said while sipping some tea she had in a mug next to her.

"All right. Well, let's go see some Spokane culture." Lisa picked up Karissa by the hand, laughing. They both walked into the kitchen and were greeted by Lisa's parents, Greta and Dan Armitage. They were a wealthy old couple who owned their own bank chain in the Northwest.

"Good morning, girls!" Greta said with a huge smile on her face. "I'm making some eggs for the big ol' lump over there, if you want some." She gestured to Dan over by the table, who was watching *College GameDay*.

"I heard that," he said jokingly.

They all laughed.

Soon after, the eggs and bacon strips were ready to eat, and they all sat around the dining table. Dan's eyes were glued to the screen. Oregon was playing Washington. Karissa wasn't really too much of a football fan, but that didn't stop Dan from his playful trash talk because she was from Oregon.

Greta told her husband to hush every time he did.

"So, Karissa, Lisa tells me you're a reporter?" Greta said while shoveling a small clump of scrambled eggs into her mouth.

"Yes, I am," Karissa said, smiling and taking a sip of her tea.

"How did you get into that line of work?"

"Well, my dad was a sports analyst for one of the local news networks back in Portland, and one day he took me to the studio, and I absolutely loved it."

"Well, I think that is just the greatest. And your husband, how did you two meet?" Greta asked while biting into a piece of bacon.

"A party, actually, when we were in college. He just came up and introduced himself. We were both kind of outsiders, I guess you could say."

"What do you mean?" Greta asked, tilting her head in confusion.

"Well, he and I both aren't really the partying type, so we just kind of gravitated toward each other, and the sparks flew."

"Oh, isn't that just adorable," Greta said, grasping her mug of coffee.

"YEAH!" Dan yelled extremely loud. "Huskies eat Ducks out here, Karissa!"

That definitely caught the ladies off guard, as all three of them flinched but then laughed afterward. Greta playfully punched Dan in the arm.

"So, what do you girls say we get out a little bit today?"

"I'd love that," Karissa said smiling.

*

Karissa was sitting in the back seat of Greta's silver SUV. Lisa was sitting up front, and Dan was back home watching Washington blow their twenty-point lead against Oregon. Karissa was looking out the window at the surrounding area. She overheard some of Lisa and Greta's conversation about gardening, but she kind of tuned them out. An occasional question was asked and answered, but then it was back to silence from Karissa. They were on the road for about twenty minutes until Greta pulled into a small parking lot in front of a little white house.

"Okay, we're here, girls!" Greta said, not holding in her excitement.

Lisa turned around and said, "Sorry, Karissa, she's just really into antiques."

Greta responded by giving Lisa's shoulder a soft punch.

"I get it," Karissa said, laughing nervously.

Lisa could tell she was still worried about Lewis. When they got out of the car, Greta complained about the "nasty weather," but Karissa didn't mind. She actually liked the climate in the Pacific Northwest.

She and Lewis both grew up in Oregon, so they were used to this weather. One summer when she was fourteen, her parents took her to Arizona because her parents didn't like the rain. After the vacation, Karissa decided that she hated the sun. She found it easier to get warm when she was cold than to cool off when she was hot. Plus, she just found the overall vibe of the rainy and foggy days to be a good one. It was always soothing. It was funny—most people thought of gloomy days as the depressing ones, but not Karissa. She found that she was calmer and happier on those days and more stressed and depressed on sunny days.

While Greta was cursing about the wet and rainy weather, Karissa was feeling quite relaxed, and when they walked inside, she was amazed by how cool the look of the house was. There were cute little knickknacks all over the place and some old-timey furniture spread around. There was one glass container that held a giant collection of old jewelry that Karissa found really interesting.

As they were looking around, they were greeted by a nice old man. The hair that remained on his head was gray, and he had a really big beard that resembled steel wool. He was petting a small orange cat that was licking itself on top of the desk that held the cash register.

"Oh, good afternoon, ladies! What can I do you for?" His smile was big and wide, as if he hadn't been expecting anyone to come in.

Karissa greeted him with a smile. "Good, thank—"

Greta cut her off. "Yes, do you have any rustic lamps? Like something a rancher or a farm boy would have?"

"Hmmm, I think I might. Follow me."

Greta began to follow him through a doorway that led to more antiques. Lisa and Karissa stayed behind and looked around.

"She really likes antique hunting, doesn't she?" Karissa said, laughing.

"Yeah, sorry about that. She didn't mean to cut you off."

"No, it's really okay. This place is pretty cool."

"How are you doing, K? Like really. Honestly."

"I'm good." She knew Lisa could see through her disguise. "I just hope he's okay. And you know Lewis. He has a tendency to get really upset about little things."

"Yeah," Lisa agreed, picking up a small ceramic ashtray. "I remember when he punched Parker in the mouth because he was hitting on you at Jack's fortieth birthday party. Lewis had just started working at the university."

"Don't remind me," Karissa said, rolling her eyes. "Parker wasn't even hitting on me. I had a little bit of cocktail sauce on my face, and he wiped it off for me."

"Honey," Lisa said, looking at her with a smirk. "That man was definitely flirting with you. Normal people would hand you a napkin."

They both laughed.

"Besides," Lisa continued, "I think that's why Jack liked him so much. All men nowadays just treat girls like change in their pocket. If they lose a penny, they still have more. But not Lewis. Jack and I could tell he truly loves you."

"Yeah." Karissa smiled to herself. She blushed a bit, thinking of the memory. Then the voices of the old man and Greta began to penetrate the women's ears. As they entered the room, Greta was holding a large rustic lamp and was super excited about it. Lisa walked over to the desk to examine the lamp her mom was losing her mind over.

Karissa looked down and thought about Lewis and how happy he made her. She wanted to go home. She wanted to see him. She wanted to hug and kiss him. She closed her eyes and smiled for a moment before she heard Greta calling her, saying they were leaving.

The girls were driving home when Greta decided she was hungry, and she took a vote to see if the rest of the car shared her feeling. Lisa did, and before Karissa could say anything, Greta turned on the highway toward downtown instead of the road back to the house. Karissa felt annoyed.

Greta was sweet, but she kept cutting Karissa off before she could even speak, and that irked her. She ignored it and pulled out her phone to text Lewis.

*Hi Lewy, just wanted to say how much I miss you, and I hope your day is going amazing. I love you.*

When they got to the diner, they were seated at a large red booth. The waitress approached and took everybody's orders. Karissa sat there with her head resting on her hand and only ordered a coffee. Greta began to complain about some lady from her country club. Karissa wasn't paying any attention, but she heard enough to know it was something about golf.

As she got her coffee, she was still lost in thought—well, more like a depression. Her eyes scanned around the restaurant until they met a person sitting in the corner. They were awfully tall and were wearing black robes and a hood.

Karissa raised her head; an expression of fear filled her face. Lisa noticed instantly and asked, "Is everything okay, K?"

Karissa, not wasting any time, stood up and stomped over to the table. When she arrived, the person was looking down.

"Hey you, asshole!" she yelled, catching the whole diner's attention. The person raised their head toward Karissa and revealed a normal man in a black sweatshirt and sweatpants. He looked at her unimpressed.

"Think you got the wrong guy, lady," he said in a gruff tone.

She realized it. "S-sorry," she stuttered.

She felt short of breath. She started walking fast, right past her booth, where Greta and Lisa were asking if she was okay. Lisa got up to follow her. The entire diner was silent and watched her storm out of the building. When she got outside, she began to panic. She fell to her knees on the sidewalk and had her anxiety attack right there in front of the diner.

It was a painful one. She couldn't breathe and felt the hands of darkness come up to grab her and pull her further into the abyss that was her mind. She felt lonely, cold, terrified. She thought of that face. The face that she saw in her nightmares. The face that had a hold on her entire self.

Lisa ran out, grabbed Karissa in her arms, and told her everything was going to be okay. She looked around and across the road while she was calming her friend down.

And in between two small buildings, she noticed somebody in a black robe standing in an alleyway. They were extremely tall. Lisa raised an eyebrow, but before she could put any more of her attention on it, the tall being faded behind a wall of fog that had made its way in front of the buildings.

*

When they returned home, Greta explained to Dan what happened as Lisa helped Karissa calm herself. The Armitages were aware of the incident back in Portland, as Lisa had told them before they arrived. They knew that this was a possibility.

Karissa was in the shower while Lisa was making her some tea. Greta and Dan were sitting on the couch watching football, though the volume was very low, and Dan was much quieter.

When Karissa entered the living room, they all looked at her with great sincerity. She stopped in her tracks and thanked them with a small smile.

"I'm sorry, Greta."

"Oh, hush now. I understand. Now, come drink some tea, and let's watch some football."

Karissa smiled, although she hated when people said they "understood." How could they? How could anyone understand the loneliness and terror she felt. Afraid of the world, afraid of herself.

She was still greatly appreciative of Greta's hospitality though, and she grabbed her tea from Lisa while she sat down on the couch. She felt a little bit more like herself, but she felt beat. Tired. And she kept thinking about why Lewis hadn't responded to her text yet.

*

It was about 7:00 p.m. when Karissa checked her phone. Still nothing from Lewis. She had texted him three times and called him four. Every time he didn't answer, she whispered to herself, "Keep going north."

Dan was asleep on the couch while Greta and Lisa were baking a cake in the kitchen. Lisa had changed their flight back to Portland to the next morning, Sunday instead of Monday. Karissa felt as though she needed to go home. She needed to get back to work. She needed to see Lewis.

She said brief goodnights to her hosts and then went to bed.

Or tried to, at least.

It took her about two hours to fall asleep, but she eventually faded into the world of dreams.

She dreamed about the day she and Lewis went to go pick out Apollo from the breeder. They wanted a child, but Karissa was unable to have one due to medical reasons. She remembered all of the visits to the doctors and all the times she cried in Lewis' arms. But she also remembered the happiness she felt when Lewis came up to her one day and said,

"This doesn't mean we can't be parents," and took her on a Saturday morning to a breeder down in Salem.

When they arrived, all of the puppies were running around—except one that wouldn't leave the Nelsons alone. Karissa lifted him up and knew he was the one.

That dream and memory was followed by more of the two of them loving the dog who became their child.

She woke up the next day to the smell of crackling bacon. She reached for her phone and saw she had no messages or missed calls from Lewis. Worried, she got out of bed, said her goodbyes to Greta and Dan, and thanked them for their kindness. She couldn't wait to get home. Lisa and Karissa entered a taxicab and headed toward the airport.

*

That night, Greta and Dan were sitting in their living room, watching more football. Dan let out a sigh and said, "Poor girl."

"I know," Greta said, looking up from her book. "Poor thing barely even ate anything while she was here."

"Did she really lose her mind while you guys were at lunch?"

"Oh, you should've seen it, Dan. She yelled at this man, stormed out of there, and fell on the sidewalk. She couldn't breathe."

"Wow. Good thing I wasn't there. I would've been embarrassed."

"Well, we didn't go through what she did. It sounds terrifying."

"Yeah, well, now we're going to get weird looks around town."

"You stop that," Greta commanded. "You were just sitting here on your butt watching that damned tv."

Dan cursed under his breath and got up with a loud sigh. He stated he was going to the bathroom and walked off into the hallway that led to it.

About ten minutes passed before Greta looked up and yelled "Are you okay in there?" while laughing.

Her laugh was cut short when she heard a loud knock on the bathroom door, making her jump out of her chair.

"Jesus! Okay, okay, I'm coming," she said, putting her book down. She hurried to the door as quickly as the old woman could. As she got closer though, she realized she couldn't see the light on from the crack under the door. She thought that was strange, but she sighed as she prepared herself to help her husband with whatever it was he needed.

"Honey?" she asked as she grabbed the door handle and turned it. When she saw inside, she froze.

A tall shadow stood there in the darkness. The man, who was about seven feet tall, lowered his head into the light of the hallway, revealing his terrifying and mutilated face. He shot his hand forward, piercing Greta's stomach. He examined her facial expression as he pulled his hand out slowly.

She stumbled back while blood leaked onto the hardwood floor. Using the wall as a crutch, she yelled for Dan until she slipped and fell in the hallway heading to their bedroom. The tall man ducked his head under the bathroom door frame.

Greta was crawling her way to the bedroom door while the tall man followed her slowly, examining, taking his time.

The bedroom door was cracked open. Once she got there, she used the last of her energy and pushed it the rest of the way while begging for Dan. However, the bedroom was covered in red spirals and Dan was lying on the bed with his jaw missing. Greta began to scream but stopped suddenly when a large foot stomped on her head, turning it to mush.

# ~ 6 ~

After the incident at the abandoned church, Lewis was sitting in the Portland City Library. He had a few books checked out. His theory was that this whole story, the two tall beings, were all involved with a cult of some kind, the symbol being engraved on both of their bodies and the fact that they looked identical. No eyelids, mouth carved from ear to ear, and insanely tall.

He knew it was also possible that the two could have just been living in the abandoned church and had done that to themselves, but Lewis didn't believe that. And because he didn't believe it, the books he was reading all included vital information about how cults operate. Why they are, what they are, and who they are.

The most interesting thing Lewis learned was how easy it was for a person to brainwash others into believing something, how they could get hundreds and thousands of others to believe it as well, all with persuasion and speech.

Cults operate with a set goal in mind. It doesn't really matter what sort of unusual belief they have; it matters what their end goal is.

One cult he read about was Heaven's Gate. The two leaders led their followers to believe that death was their way of becoming immortal, that they could be transported to a UFO following a comet. Mass suicide followed.

The next cult he read about was the Fall River cult, where a man made everybody believe he was the spawn of Satan and demanded human sacrifice during his rituals.

Lewis believed that if a cult did exist around the two tall beings, there had to be an overall goal and belief. And, as much as he hated to admit it, he was afraid to find out what that end goal was.

He began to feel a twitch in his face. A ringing in his ears. An itch at the base of his skull. It was stronger this time. His head began to pound as he closed his eyes in pain, but once they were shut he saw quick, flashing images.

A burning tree.

A large black church.

Snow on the ground with hints of blood.

Then, suddenly, the images stopped.

Lewis shook his head as the strange symptoms quickly faded away. He inspected the books that sat on the desk in front of him, but he decided they were not enough. He then pulled his phone out of his pocket and noticed the large number of notifications he had.

They were all from Karissa. There were three missed texts and four missed calls from her.

He read the texts.

The first one had been sent while he and Bolton were investigating the abandoned chapel.

*Hi Lewy, just wanted to say how much I miss you, and I hope your morning is going amazing. I love you.*

The next one was sent two hours later.

*Tried calling, no answer. You okay?*

The last one was an hour after that.

*Lewis, what the hell is going on? I'm worried sick. It's Saturday, so I know you aren't at work. Lisa and I are coming home in the morning.*

Lewis sat there staring at the messages. He knew that if Karissa found out about him working with Bolton, she'd instantly stop him. Or, worse, she'd ask to help.

It wasn't that he wouldn't want her help, but he figured the last thing she needed to worry about was him, so he texted her back.

*Hey baby, there is no need for you to come home tomorrow, please stay and enjoy your trip. I am fine, just been a busy day. Love you.*

He then packed up his things and proceeded to go home.

*

Bolton was back at the station, waiting for all of the evidence to come back from the church. When he got the text that it had arrived, he walked to the evidence locker.

Jane, who worked in forensics, walked him through everything they'd found. There were multiple leather books with spirals stitched into the covers. The books didn't have any writing in them at all. Just random symbols. Next, Jane showed him an arsenal of rusty knives, hatchets, and a scythe. She told him they'd been found in the back room of the church.

Next, they found a number of stained maps. Some of the city of Portland, another of the Pacific Northwest, and another of the United States. These maps were stained with either blood, bile, or bodily fluids—they weren't quite sure yet.

Finally, there was a dark tan envelope that was sealed shut. Bolton asked Jane if anybody else had seen the evidence yet, to which she replied no. He grabbed the envelope and opened it up. It was a letter.

*Dear Angels,*

*It is almost time. We shall rise and take our place in this world. In HIS world. The power of the righteous is in our hands. Rejoice my children, the Cleansing is nigh!*

*Your father,*

*Calvin*

"Well, looks like we found our cult leader," Bolton said. He felt this would be a good time to speak to Byrd, as the evidence obviously showed there was more to this story, that the case was definitely not closed.

He headed back to his office with the books and the letter, and he called Agent Phil from the FBI.

Phil answered the phone like he always did: "Yyyyellow?"

"Yeah, Phil, it's Bolton. Listen, we are one hundred percent dealing with a cult here. I got a bunch of pictures I'm sending you. Have you found anything out about our little symbol?"

"No, not at all, man. There is no known religion that even uses a spiral in their worship, so we are dealing with something new here."

"Well, I got a name: Calvin. And if I was a betting man, I'd bet he's our leader."

"How'd you manage to find that?"

Bolton explained how he'd found an abandoned church in downtown Portland, how he'd killed another tall man with a mutilated face wearing the exact same clothes as the first man. He then sent over pictures of all of the evidence.

The only thing he left out was that a young University psychology professor helped him.

"Whoa, whoa!" Phil said as he looked over the photos of the book pages with the symbols.

"What?" Bolton asked, concerned.

"Dude, these are freaking Nordic runes!"

"Runes? What do you mean?"

"It's the alphabet of, like, Vikings and shit." Phil sounded very excited.

"Okay, why would they be using runes?"

"Well, runes were an alphabet, yeah, but if you carved some in specific patterns, then apparently they'd hold supernatural powers of protection."

"Wait, powers? What are you talking about, man?" Bolton asked, confused as all hell.

"Yeah, like, for example, if a warrior carved some runes on his sword or shield or something before battle, then supposedly Odin or one of the Norse gods would give them extra strength while they fought."

"Okay, so," Bolton started, "let's look into any cults that deal with Nordic runes."

"Yeah," Phil exclaimed. "And be on the lookout for any more runes."

"Listen, Phil, before I let you go, I need you to see if there's a connection with the Patrick Hopkins murder and any others like it. I'm talking extremely mutilated bodies that have been torn apart or stabbed or something like that. I haven't seen these guys use a gun yet, so we can cross that off for now."

"Yeah, I'll check to see. I'm sure we would've noticed something like this though."

"Just check for me, please. Let me know when you have something."

Bolton said his goodbyes and told Phil he was going to see Byrd.

He knocked on Byrd's office door and greeted him happily. He knew he was finally going to get backup and justice for the officers who died on the bridge. He had irrefutable evidence this case was bigger than they'd thought.

"So," Bolton smirked. "I'd like to do a search of the surrounding buildings to see if there is anything else like this down there."

"You just got out of that; you sure you don't want to rest for a little? Go ahead, go home. We got this," Byrd said, obviously irritated.

"No. You messed with this case for too long, and if it wasn't for me, you'd still have another person like that in this city. And who knows, maybe you have more out there. Don't worry, I'll find out, because obviously this case is reopening,"

Bolton said, laughing. "Federal agents are coming to back me up in this case because lord knows you aren't."

Byrd scoffed and took a sip of his coffee. Bolton threw a manila folder on his desk and stormed out. Byrd opened it and saw pictures of the evidence they'd collected. Including the letter.

Bolton continued toward his office and thought about everything going on. He believed he no longer needed Lewis, since he knew he was going to get more help on the case with the evidence he found. As he sat down, he pulled out his phone and brought up Lewis' number. He did know, however, that Lewis probably wouldn't take this very well, just judging by his previous behavior.

Lewis picked up almost immediately.

"Bolton! Glad to hear from you, what did you guys find?" he said, very excited.

"Lewis, we have to talk."

Lewis waited patiently for Bolton to continue.

"I got backup from the bureau. It's coming soon. So this means I can't have you working with me anymore. It is just unprofessional to have a civilian on a case. But I wanted to let you know how appreciative I am of your help, and now I have the resources to solve this case."

"Okay. No problem."

"Wait," Bolton said, surprised. "That's it?"

"Yeah. Bolton, you got to remember, I'm a psychology professor. I know how these things go down. You got backup, so now maybe you will actually solve this case. It's all good."

Before Bolton could say anything more, Lewis thanked him for his time, then hung up. Bolton sat there at his desk. Lewis had told him that he was okay with not being on the case. He shook it off and didn't think much of it.

*

Lewis returned home after a few hours at the library. He walked into his bathroom, turned the shower on, then proceeded to take off the jacket the police gave him after the incident at the church. He noticed he still had a little blood on his undershirt. He cursed to himself under his breath.

After getting in the shower, he felt the strange itch in his brain again. It was softer this time, like a small buzz. He looked up and felt the water pouring down on his face as he thought about the wild events that occurred on that Saturday.

Then, the water turned into the drool and bile that had leaked from the mouth of the evil being, and for a moment Lewis was back in the church. He heard Bolton's gun pop loudly and felt the brains and blood from the being splatter on his face.

He woke from his trance.

He sighed.

After he got dressed, Lewis decided to take a short walk around his neighborhood. He slid on his shoes, stepped out the front door, and felt the brisk air hit his face.

It was soothing.

Calming.

As he walked, he thought about Karissa. His beautiful and incredible wife. He loved her. He thought about his job.

The one where he got to talk about his passions. He loved teaching.

He then thought about this case and the nights he'd stayed up helping Karissa through panic attacks. The nights the twitch in his head would wake him and force him to think of nothing other than the tall beings, what they did. What they might do.

He realized this case was eating away at him. But he finally got Bolton to do his job and get backup. With his help, Bolton now had the necessary tools to handle the situation.

Lewis felt a small moment of pure relaxation. Karissa was coming home the next morning, and he felt happiness. He cracked a smile and was ready to give up the case. It wasn't his to crack, and he knew it.

When he finally decided to head back to the house, he practically skipped home. Things were looking up and he couldn't stop smiling. His main goal for the next day? Give his wife more love than she could even imagine.

As he finally got back to his house and opened the front door, his foot hit something. He looked down.

A black envelope lay on his floor.

*How did this get here?* Lewis thought.

He picked it up and found a red wax seal on the envelope. It held the shape of a spiral. The itch returned to his skull, like he'd just run full sprint into a brick wall.

He examined it for a moment. His first thought was to burn it. To just be done with the whole thing.

His eye twitched.

His next thought was to call Bolton, but his ears began to ring. The only thing that stopped the itch was when he held the note with both hands and looked at it.

He had to open it.

He took the letter to the kitchen table and turned on a small lamp in the corner. He looked at the seal one more time and took a deep breath before he popped it open.

Inside was a letter on red paper. The writing was in cursive and written in black ink. He squinted and examined the red paper. When he turned the letter around, he noticed there was a watermark.

It looked like an official seal.

There was a ring surrounding a spiral, and there were three words above the ring that read, "The Angels of Artemis." Lewis flipped the paper around again and began to read the words.

*Dear Mr. Nelson,*

*I have been tasked with informing you that our father, Calvin, requested your assistance with the Cleansing. It is obvious you are the one we have been looking for. You are to rendezvous with me eight miles east of Mount Hood. You will need to walk a short distance and arrive at a small cabin. Knock on the door three times. All of your questions will be answered soon.*

*The time is among us, brother.*

*Your friend,*

*Reggie*

Lewis felt a chill radiate through his spine. He felt bile rise into his throat. He ran to the toilet in his bathroom and vomited.

His eyes were wide as he walked back over to the letter. The itch in his brain was now stronger than it had ever been, causing his eye to twitch, as well as the corner of his mouth.

*Okay, Lewis,* he thought to himself. *Call Bolton and tell him about the letter. Your part in this is over. The FBI will take care of everything.*

There were a few moments of hesitation.

He let out a sigh and grabbed the letter as he walked to his closet, pulling out a black leather jacket. He packed a backpack of extra clothes, snacks, and water, as he had no idea how long he would be gone. He went to his drawer, pulled out his Magnum and extra ammo, and stored them in his backpack as well. He swung it over his shoulder and grabbed his keys as he proceeded to enter his car and drive off into the midnight sun.

*

Karissa was sitting next to Lisa on the plane. It was a crisp but sunny Sunday morning all across the Pacific Northwest. The rain from the previous night had created a dense fog.

Lisa was asking the flight attendant for some water, while Karissa was looking at old pictures on her iPad. When Lisa's drink order was finished, she caught a glimpse of the photos her friend was looking at. The photo she saw was one of Lewis holding Apollo when he was just a puppy.

Karissa locked the iPad screen.

"Are you okay?" Lisa asked sincerely.

"Yeah," Karissa replied, looking out the window. "I'm just worried about him. Ever since that night, Lewis hasn't been the same."

"What do you mean?" Lisa said, receiving her water.

"He's just been very distant. I mean, obviously he's been my rock, and he's helped in any way he can, but for some reason, he just doesn't seem like himself."

"Any reason in particular?"

"Well...yeah. This is going to be kind of dark."

Lisa nodded her head, making it known that she was ready.

"It was one of the first nights after that freak came to our house," Karissa started, "and I had an anxiety attack. I felt depressed, and every time I closed my eyes, all I saw was that horrifying face pressed against the window. I saw him everywhere. When I was at work, when I was watching TV, when I blinked—all I saw was that man's face."

She paused for a brief moment then continued. "Anyways, I got low that night. Real low. I knew where Lewis hid the gun, so I went and grabbed it and... I put it to my head."

"Karissa..." Lisa said in a low tone.

"Lewis got home before I could do anything," Karissa continued. "He walked into our room and saw that. He sprinted to me and swatted the gun away from me. He broke down in tears and held me close to him. As I started to calm down, I looked into his eyes, and he told me that I was the most important thing in the world to him and that he'll never let me go. He told me to keep going north. Find the motivation to keep going, because if I ended my life, then that freak would win. And it hit me. I had to be stronger. That was the first night I was able to actually close my eyes in peace. I knew he was right there with me. Lewis could protect me from anything, even myself."

"Oh, my god," Lisa said. "I had no idea."

"Well, that night, everything kind of changed for the both of us. I knew I had to be stronger for him, and so I decided to make that change. But something else happened that night. At about 3:00 a.m., I woke up, and he was gone. I heard some loud noises in the garage, and I went to go look. I opened the door a bit and saw he was on his hands and knees. He was moving up and down, almost like he was praying to someone. I asked him what he was doing, and he didn't say anything. I started to get scared, but I walked up to him anyway and noticed his eyes were closed. When I asked him what he was doing again, he just said the word 'cleanse' and fell over. It was like he was sleepwalking."

"Oh, my god," Lisa said, putting her hand over her mouth. "Did you talk to him about it?"

"No. I brushed it off for a day or two, until I caught him doing it again. He did it two more times. Instead of talking to him, I thought about what he was doing for me. I almost killed myself, and he stopped it. So, I realized I needed to do the same thing for him, as obviously that experience was terrifying for the both of us. I needed to be there for him. I started telling him to keep going north as well, and it seemed to calm him down. I realized we both needed each other, but we never really talked about it. I think we both just thought it was a good idea to forget it."

"Yeah, I think that was the right call," Lisa said, sipping her water.

"Actually, now I don't think that was such a good idea. I never should've left. He responded late last night, but the way his behavior changed since I left was just such a shock. I need to be there for him just as much as he's there for me."

"I'm sure he'll be there when you get home. And if he happens not to, or if something seems strange, why don't you call that detective? The good-looking one on TV."

"Yeah, I guess I can."

"Now, let's just enjoy the flight, okay? You'll be home as soon as you know it."

Lisa laid her head back after sipping the last of her drink. Karissa looked outside the window and let out a sigh. Her mind was racing.

*

It was after midnight on that cool, moonlit evening, and Lewis had parked his car at a rest stop just off the highway. He grabbed his backpack and threw it over his shoulder after taking out his flashlight and turning it on. His Magnum was fully loaded and tucked inside the back of his jeans, tightened into position by his belt.

Believe it or not, Lewis didn't like guns. Not at all. But his dad taught him how to use one when he was younger. He remembered waking up at the crack of dawn to his father dragging him out of bed to go hunting. One day, when Lewis was about thirteen, he and his dad were out in the mountains, looking for elk.

Well, young Lewis decided he didn't want to kill things anymore. He had an argument with his dad, and he took off. After a couple of hours, he realized he was lost, and he began to yell for his dad. He lost his footing on a hillside and tumbled down into a river, where there just happened to be a black bear trying to catch some fish.

Lewis screamed loudly as the black bear began to walk toward him. If it weren't for a bullet from his dad's gun, he could've been mauled.

As Lewis sat there crying, looking at nothing but the dead bear in the river, his dad ran to him and grabbed his face. He looked at him in the eyes and told his son, "Lewis, you need to understand. Sometimes, we have to fight to survive. You may not want to seek out death, but sometimes it comes knocking at the door, and you need to be prepared for that moment. Always be prepared."

Lewis remembered his father's words as he looked up at the mountain before him in the moonlight.

*Eight miles east of the mountain*, he thought to himself.

He saw a small trail that was overgrown and practically hidden.

*Guess I'll start here.*

He felt some mist on his face, but it was still a pretty clear and nice evening. When he looked up at the sky, the moon was humungous. Because of that, he could see Mount Hood and its glistening white cap of snow without trouble. The mountain towered before him. He turned off his flashlight, as he could see everything without it.

Lewis walked without making a sound or even thinking a thought for a while. He was practically going through the motions. It was almost like his mind had not caught up with his body yet.

He kept walking.

His feet began to ache, but there was no worry for what time it was or how long he had been walking for. He just kept walking. One foot after the other.

Suddenly, he tripped over something, and that made him snap out of his trance.

"Damn it!" he exclaimed.

He looked down at what had tripped him. The dirt path had become a walkway of cobblestone. He got up off the ground with his eyes open wide. He looked around to see if anyone was there but found nothing.

After a brief moment of hesitation, he began to walk the pathway. After about fifteen minutes, he came over a small hill, where he saw a small orange light.

He froze.

This was it.

A cabin in the middle of the woods.

*Well, you already came this far*, he thought to himself.

He continued. When he got closer, he could see the light was flickering. Most likely a lantern, the way it made the shadows of trees dance around it. With every step, he was reminded of the evil being's mutilated face and teeth as its mouth leaked saliva over him before Bolton shot it dead. He wondered if that was what was waiting for him inside the house, then he wondered if he should turn around. But his feet kept moving.

Before his mind caught up with his body, he was already at the wooden door. He looked around. The lantern was now beside him, and it lit up the surrounding area. It was a nice cabin. There was gleaming metal framework on the door. It looked as though the cabin was owned by somebody with a lot of money.

Lewis raised his hand, preparing to knock on the door. He hesitated for a second then sighed. He remembered that the note told him to knock three times, and he did.

*Knock, knock, knock.*

After a few seconds of pure anxiety, an old man opened the door. To Lewis' surprise, he looked like a regular old man. No mutilated face, no black robe, and he was actually shorter than Lewis.

The old man was wearing a red button-down shirt with black pants. He greeted Lewis with a friendly smile.

"So, you must be Lewis!" the old man said, happy as could be.

Lewis nodded in confirmation.

"Come in, come in! My name is Reggie."

Lewis followed Reggie inside and looked around nervously. The cabin was lit by the fireplace. There were a few candles around, and Lewis noticed the cabin smelled like fresh strawberries. There were three deer heads mounted above the fireplace, and in front of the crackling fire was a huge black bear rug. The cabin was just as nice on the inside as it was on the outside, if not more so.

Reggie gestured for Lewis to sit down on a brown couch while he sat in a black recliner. "I'm sure you have plenty of questions, Lewis," the old man said, smiling. "You have nothing to worry about. They'll all be answered here."

"Okay, yeah, that'd be great," Lewis said, chuckling, trying to act as calm and friendly as possible. He knew that if he acted strangely, things might not go so well. He needed to play along.

"Well, let me start with the basics," Reggie began. "I am part of The Angels of Artemis. We are a group of individuals who have been chosen by King Artemis to carry out his will."

Lewis tried his best to keep his friendly smile even though now he wanted to get out of that cabin as quickly as possible. But he needed answers.

"You probably haven't heard of us, although you have noticed us. That is precisely the reason you are here."

Reggie cleared his throat. "See, our organization is spread out across the world. We listen to the words of our King, and we find those who are unworthy of his world and cleanse them of it. And one night, when one of our Angels was cleansing a man of his dishonesty and lust, he just so happened to cross paths with you. He could've cleansed your soul there, but for some reason, he didn't. He followed you to your house and gave you quite the scare," Reggie said, chuckling.

Lewis laughed along nervously.

"I'm sorry about that," Reggie continued. "They are supposed to wear a sort of sack over their face when selecting and large pointed hood when they are idle."

"Are Angels the tall..." Lewis paused. He wanted to say "freaks" but instead said, "People?"

"Why yes, they are quite tall, aren't they?" Reggie said, chuckling.

"So, what does this have to do with me?" Lewis asked with a straight face. His nerves began to calm down as he remembered he was there for answers. And sure enough, he was getting them.

"Well, everything Lewis," the old man said. "Our Angels are specifically modified to track down those unworthy of Artemis' world and release them of their sinful lives, just like those who wronged him once before. However, we have never once had an Angel not carry out what they were designed to and stalk a soul for a long period of time. It is usually a quick process. The Angel discovers who is unworthy and then stalks them before cleansing them. Then they retreat."

"Okay, so then why did that *Angel* not kill me?" Lewis asked.

"Lewis," Reggie said, looking into his eyes. "You are the chosen one."

Lewis let out a small laugh and became irritated. "I'm the chosen one because one of your people followed me home, killed my dog, and traumatized my wife? I'm the chosen one of your cult because one of your 'hitmen of Artemis' decided to let me live?"

Reggie became angry. He smacked the end table that sat next to his recliner with his fist, and it made a loud bang. "WE ARE NOT A CULT!"

Lewis' cocky attitude instantly dropped, and his nerves began to rise again.

"I apologize, Lewis," Reggie said, instantly going back to normal. "I just wanted to inform you that we are not a cult. We are chosen by the one true King, Artemis. We are not insane like these others. And yes, our Angels are bred to cleanse those who are unworthy. In the hundreds of years that we have been active, we have never once seen anything like what happened to you."

*Hundreds of years?* Lewis thought to himself before he continued to play along.

"I don't know, Reggie; I'm just a college professor, I'm no messiah," Lewis said, frightened at the kind old man who'd just lost his temper and gone back to normal like nothing happened. He knew he had to act interested even though he believed this old man was crazy.

"Have you felt the ticks yet?" Reggie asked in a cold, lifeless voice.

Lewis froze. Chills spread all over his body. "W-what?" Lewis asked, his eyes widening.

"When you are chosen by Artemis, he sends ticks to certain areas to push you in a direction. He is trapped, Lewis. In an unforgiving world, and those ticks are his way of leading you down the right path. It is your destiny. When the tick gets stronger, you know you are doing the right thing."

Lewis was caught off guard; he felt vulnerable. He didn't know what to say or do. He was glued to the couch.

"Listen, Lewis. Something is coming. Something we were unaware of until we met you. We have been able to cleanse the world, but only by small amounts. And it seems the more we cleanse, the more imperfect people are brought into this world. But we have been preparing for the final piece of the puzzle. And because of your continued encounters with the Angels, we now know it is time to finally put that piece into place."

Lewis swallowed hard as Reggie continued.

"We have spent hundreds of years creating outposts. Each outpost is equipped with its own Angels and what they need to survive. Just like the one that you destroyed with the detective."

Sweat dripped down Lewis' brow.

"But no matter. We have thousands more. Our people are everywhere and nowhere. A time of righteousness is coming. He is coming. The Cleansing is nigh."

Lewis was at a loss for words. He finally understood. He just so happened to pass an outpost that night when Patrick Hopkins was killed—or "cleansed," as Reggie put it. The "Angel" followed Lewis back to his home and proceeded to kill Apollo and traumatize Karissa. Bolton then killed that Angel on the bridge.

Lewis had felt the "ticks" grow stronger since then. They kept him up at night. They led him to the church where he had his second encounter with an Angel. They led him to obsess over this case. The ticks led him to come to this cabin in the middle of nowhere. The Angels of Artemis were going to kill everyone that this Artemis didn't see worthy of his world. This was a bigger cult than Lewis had ever seen. The most dangerous one.

"And this cabin, and you—why are you here? Is this an outpost?"

"No," Reggie said, chuckling. "I am simply here for you, Lewis. I was put here as a young man, and I have been waiting for this very moment for a long time. In fact, I am what you call a recruiter. And for hundreds of years, we recruiters have waited for the chosen one. We are born into this role, migrate to where we are needed, and then we pass on to the next one until the chosen one is, well, chosen," he said with a laugh.

"You mean, you've been here for years?"

"Precisely. There have been recruiters set up all around the world since the first age of Artemis. I have been here since I was old enough to talk. Waiting for you, Lewis."

"So, where do we go from here?" Lewis asked, trying to process and also learn more information.

Reggie got up from his recliner and walked over to his kitchen.

"Well, Lewis, everybody has a job in the Angels of Artemis, and when that job is finished, they must cleanse themselves. You, however, your job is to go to Blackgate. It is our main village, in Iceland. It is about seventeen miles east of Dalvik."

"You said Iceland?" Lewis asked while watching Reggie open a drawer and reach his hand in.

"Yes. When you arrive at the gates, you will ask for Calvin. He is our righteous leader and speaker of Artemis. Do you understand your role, Lewis?"

"Yeah, I think I got it. What are you doing?" Lewis noticed a strange look in Reggie's eyes.

"Like I stated earlier," Reggie said, smiling. "We all have jobs, and mine was to give you the information you need to arrive and become the vessel of our King."

Reggie pulled out a large revolver from the drawer and put the barrel in his mouth.

"Wait! Reg—"

Reggie pulled the trigger and painted the wall behind him with blood. Lewis sat there in shock for a moment.

Then he screamed in agony.

*

Karissa arrived at the Portland International Airport around noon. She had been quiet the entire flight. Lisa was talking to somebody she knew while they waited for their bags at the baggage claim when she noticed Karissa staring off into the distance at the spectacular Mount Hood.

"Hey, you all right?" Lisa asked, walking over to her.

"Yeah, the mountain is beautiful today," Karissa said in a sad and shaky voice.

"Jack texted me that he's here, so we just got to get our bags and we can go, okay?"

Karissa nodded and walked toward the baggage carousel. When the girls' bags arrived, they picked them up and walked to the exit. Sure enough, Jack was sitting in his car off to the side of the pickup area. When he saw them, he got out and hugged his wife, said hi to Karissa, and helped them put their bags in the trunk of his car.

The drive home was quiet. No questions were asked, no stories were told, just light and short commentary of things they saw as they drove by. When they arrived at the Nelson house, Lewis' car wasn't parked in the driveway like it usually was. Karissa let out a sigh and looked down. Jack offered to stay and help her if she needed anything, but she declined. She told the Garcias thanks and walked up to the door.

It was unlocked.

She walked in and looked around. Nothing seemed out of place, but her guard was up. She made her way to the bedroom and put her bag down. She then walked into the bathroom and let out a small gasp—the mirror above the sink was gone. The glass had been cleaned up, but it was frightening to see.

"Lewy...what the hell happened?" she said, shaking her head in sadness. She walked out into the kitchen and started yelling for her husband. She became angry, as the situation was worsening. She opened the sliding glass door to the backyard and screamed for her husband one last time.

"LEWIS!" She yelled so loud her voice broke.

She shook her head and stormed inside, then proceeded to pull out Detective Bolton's card. She didn't hesitate as she dialed the number.

After a few rings, he answered.

"Detective Bolton," he said, sounding busy.

"Hello, Detective. Sorry to bother you. It's Karissa Nelson."

"Oh, hello, Mrs. Nelson. What can I do for you?"

"It's Lewis."

Bolton froze. He thought about the day before, when he allowed a civilian to help with an investigation and almost got him killed. "What about him?"

"I wasn't able to reach him while I was away, so I came home, and he's not here. The mirror in the bathroom is broken too."

Bolton swore under his breath. He knew if anything happened to Lewis, he would be responsible. "Okay, when was the last time you heard from him?"

"Yesterday morning. He was acting strange, and then that was it. I got a text from him too but it was just weird. I know I shouldn't worry too much, but he's been different since that night. I guess I didn't want to admit it, but I should've."

"How do you mean?" Bolton asked, concerned.

"I caught him sleepwalking, I think. I don't really know, but then I leave for one day, and the contact I did have with him just felt...off. I shouldn't have left."

Bolton didn't know if he should tell her what happened. It might ease her to know that he was with her husband, and had even spoken to him the night before, but it also might freak her out to know that he let Lewis come with him on the investigation.

"Can you come over here, Bolton?" Karissa asked. "I want to know what you think. I'll tell you everything I know."

"Yeah, I'll be there shortly."

Bolton packed up his things and headed out.

*

When Bolton arrived at the Nelsons', he was greeted by Karissa standing in the doorway, holding a mug.

"Good afternoon, Mrs. Nelson," Bolton said with a smile.

"Hello, Andrew." She looked very tired.

Karissa led Bolton to the dinner table. The same table where Lewis demanded he help Bolton with the case. He noticed a cup of coffee waiting for him.

They both sat down.

"Thank you, Mrs. Nelson."

"Please, call me Karissa."

Bolton nodded. "How was your flight?"

"Good," she said, sighing.

Bolton could tell she wasn't in the mood for small talk. She wanted to know where her husband was, and honestly, so did he. "Okay, Karissa, I'm not going to waste any of your time. You said Lewis was sleepwalking? How many times?"

"I don't know, but a few. And I wouldn't really call it that. It was more of a sleep-praying, if that makes any sense."

"Can you explain?"

"I caught him in the garage a couple times on his hands and knees, like he was praying to somebody. He kept saying the word 'cleanse.' I have no idea what it means."

"Cleanse?" Bolton said with a confused look.

That look of confusion lasted about a moment before his eyes widened. He remembered the note that they found after their encounter with the tall being.

*The cleansing is nigh.*

"Shit," he said under his breath.

"What? Does that mean something?"

Bolton looked ashamed. He looked into Karissa's eyes and knew he had to tell her. "Lewis was helping me with the case."

"What?" she said, shocked.

"When you left, he came to my office on Friday and asked me about the man who came to your house. He actually made a scene and stormed out when I said the department was closing the case. We then got the autopsy back and found a spiral engraved on the guy's sternum. I came to your house that night and asked him if he knew anything. That was all I was there for."

He stopped talking, but the look in Karissa's eyes forced him to continue.

"He knew I didn't have backup for this, so he decided he was going to help me. The next morning, we met downtown, where Patrick Hopkins died. He found an abandoned church, and we went inside. Another tall thing was in there, along with other evidence that is now helping in the case. Then it jumped on Lewis, but I shot and killed the freak. Afterward, with the stuff we recovered from that church, I was able to get the FBI involved and told Lewis he couldn't help anymore. He said okay, and that was it."

Bolton could practically see the steam coming off Karissa's head. "Are you kidding me, Bolton? You brought him into your case because you couldn't do it yourself? You're an FBI agent, and he's a college professor. A teacher! You could've gotten him killed!"

"I know. But without him, I never would've looked in that church. The commissioner here didn't bother to try because he wants to forget the case happened, and I had no idea it was even there."

Karissa scoffed. "When did you talk to Lewis last?"

"Last night around five."

"Okay, well I got a message from him about an hour after that, but he never answered my other calls, including the two I made this morning. Where the hell could he have gone?" she asked.

Bolton could tell she was mad at him but was more focused on finding her husband. "Were you supposed to come home today?" he asked after a moment of silence.

"No, tomorrow. But since he wasn't returning my calls, Lisa and I came home today."

"Lisa...Garcia?"

"Yeah, do you know her?"

"I met her husband Jack a while ago. Where did you guys go?"

"Does this have anything to do with Lewis?"

"Yes, I want to get the full story," he said while pulling out a notepad.

"Well, Lisa took me to her parents' place in Spokane for the weekend because I've been having some issues with anxiety and depression since that night."

"Okay, and who are her parents?"

"Dan and Greta Armitage. They live in a really big house on a lake."

"Okay, well maybe Lewis wasn't planning on you coming back today, and that's why he left. Why he didn't return your calls, I don't know. I also have no idea why he would decide to just leave. The broken mirror might have been him. You said he was having issues as well, and so I think he might've done that himself since there's no sign of any other damage, no forced entry, and nothing seems stolen."

"But where could he have gone?" Karissa asked.

"Honestly, I have no idea."

## ~ 7 ~

It was a snowy Sunday morning in Chicago. Claire's luxurious apartment was rooted in the dead center of the city. She got out of her bed, stretching loudly, then proceeded to happily skip to her kitchen and begin making some coffee as she called for her cat. After she put a scoop of catnip into the bowl, she laid it on the floor.

She continued calling for her cat, but he never came. He always did, especially when the sound of the bowl rattling on the floor reached his little ears. She started looking around her house and couldn't find him. Her mood changed in an instant.

"Benny!" she called out nervously. She walked into the hallway and looked around—nothing. She felt afraid, but she couldn't stay and look for him, as she was meeting her sister for a coffee at a café close by. Claire got dressed and left her apartment after one more quick trip around the apartment to see if she could find Benny. And again, nothing.

"Damn it," she said before leaving her apartment.

As she walked out of her building, she noticed a few police cars and an ambulance cutting off her path to the café. It seemed to be a single car that had slid into the other lane and crashed into the median because of the ice.

Claire decided to find another route to the café, so she walked down the alley next to her building. She typically didn't like alleyways, but the sun was up, even if it was hidden behind a thick white sheet of clouds.

As she walked further down the alley, she felt a chill rise through her spine. She felt as though somebody was watching her. Claire looked up at the two buildings that surrounded her and noticed a person was looking down at her from a window. She got a little freaked out but realized she was close to the end of the alley. She started walking at a faster pace, but before she could get to the end, a horrible smell hit her nostrils and made her instantly queasy. She was afraid to look anywhere, as she thought there would be human waste from a homeless man.

She couldn't help herself, however, as she slowed her pace and looked at where the smell was coming from. In the corner of the alley, she saw her cat. He was ripped in two. She wanted to scream loudly, but before she could, a large hand wrapped around her mouth, keeping it shut. She felt the hot breath of a person behind her. He put his disfigured mouth next to her ear, and, after a small silence, he moaned an otherworldly sound then proceeded to snap her neck.

*

That Monday morning, Agent Phil was looking at the multiple files and papers he had spread across his desk. His eyes widened as he noticed something.

"Holy shit..." Agent Phil said. He emerged from his office quickly, ran to the FBI director's office, and barged in. "I've figured it out!"

"Okay, get Bolton on the phone," the director said, showing signs of intrigue.

*

On that crisp Monday morning, Bolton was at the police station trying to put all the pieces together. He had photos and information posted on a large board in his office. He was cursing to himself at all the information he didn't have. Little did he know, he was going to get what he asked for.

The phone in his office rang.

"Detective Bolton."

"Bolton, I'm here with the director," Phil said, sounding excited.

"Hello, sir."

"Hello, Detective Bolton. Agent Phil seems to have some information for you about this...I believe we are calling it a cult," the director said, his voice raspy. He wanted to hear this as well.

"Okay, Bolton, I've figured it out."

"Figured what out, the symbol?"

"The cult in general. Hear me out, a spiral can symbolize harmony, or a new beginning. It can also symbolize the connection of god with his followers and the energy of space."

"Wait, space?"

"Well, I don't believe these tall guys who keep showing up and this Calvin fella have anything to do with space but..."

"Wait, what about Heaven's Gate? They believed a space-ship was following a comet. They worshiped some weird space idea like that; why couldn't these guys do the same?" Bolton asked, surprised at himself as he remembered the details of what Lewis had told him.

"Could be, but a spiral means more. If you drew a spiral on paper, you'd start with a central dot, correct? You'd then continue the line until it becomes a spiral, and you can make it however big you wish. So, the spiral itself shows that there is one person, most likely this Calvin, who started this. My theory is that he's the dot. He was able to grow this cult around whatever idea he created, and boom! Now they could be anywhere."

"Okay," Bolton said, trying to gather all the info.

"The questions is," Agent Phil continued, "what is the idea that this Calvin is making all of these people believe? What is their end goal? Well, I did some digging, and I think that they carry out whatever wish this Calvin guy has—and by that, I mean kill, in very specific ways. I'm talking, like, kill to please whoever is in charge or maybe who they're worshiping, if they are worshipping anyone, that is."

"So, like sacrifices to a god basically."

"Yes, and that's not all. I've been able to connect a few murders."

"All in Portland?" Bolton asked, concerned.

"No. All across America."

Bolton shot up in his chair. "No way," he said, surprised.

"Okay, so Patrick Hopkins was murdered a month ago. You found him without his limbs. Both arms and legs were torn off, absolutely mutilated. Sure, you killed the suspect, and the department there wanted to close the case and move on. But, as you dug up more of this cultlike behavior, especially with the spiral, I looked into the background of Patrick Hopkins. I wanted to see if there was any reason for a cult to go after him. I found that Patrick was involved in an affair with a much younger woman. If this cult follows a strict set of rules, then maybe these tall guys go out and find and kill those who don't follow them. The Spokane Police Department also found two deceased elderly people in their home this morning, showing signs that they were killed by 'a very strong person.'"

That caught Bolton off guard, and he interrupted Agent Phil. "Wait, did you say Spokane? Elderly people? What were their names?"

"Uh, Greta and Dan Armitage. Why?"

"Holy shit." Bolton thought back to his conversation with Karissa.

"What is it, Detective?" the director asked, curious.

"It's my next lead. Keep going." Bolton furiously pulled out a pen and paper and started writing down everything Agent Phil was saying.

"Okay," Phil continued, "Greta and Dan were money launderers. That's how they could afford their house on the lake. Proverbs 15:27 says: 'He who is greedy for gain troubles his own house, but he who hates bribes will live.' And both of them were killed in their house. There are murders like this all over the country, Bolton. I could give you ten more examples of this shit. There's one in Texas, one in Rhode Island...they're everywhere."

"Okay, but that's assuming the cult has a Christian belief, right?"

"Not exactly," Phil said, shaking his head. "I'm looking for murders where the victims have done bad things, in case the cult's rules of who's allowed to live follow that of the Bible's and getting into Heaven, you know?"

Bolton agreed before Agent Phil continued.

"The reason I am connecting these murders is because of the victims' backgrounds, how they died, and if any suspects have been found. All of these cases I put together share those similarities. The victim has done something in their past, they were found mutilated, and are now cold cases with no suspect."

Bolton wrote everything down then said, "Wait, who's the girl that Patrick was having an affair with, do we know? She'd easily be another target if the cult hasn't gotten to her yet. If Patrick wasn't worthy of living according to the cult, she wouldn't be either."

"Uh..." Phil looked at his files once more. "Claire Fox. Apparently, after Patrick died, she moved to Chicago. She lives in an apartment in the city."

"Okay, let's start there. We need to get people over there now," Bolton said.

"On it," the director said, snapping his fingers to another agent outside the office.

"Phil, thank you so much. Let me know if you find anything more!" Bolton said happily then hung up the phone.

*

Detective Bolton was in his SUV, driving quickly through downtown Portland. He was heading to the Nelsons' house as quickly as possible. While he was driving, he picked his phone up and called Karissa.

She answered after a brief moment. "Hello, Detective," she said calmly.

"Karissa! You need to stay on guard! I'll be there shortly."

"Wait, what?" She heard the panic in his voice. "What's wrong?"

"The cult is targeting your family! Get to the dining room and stay behind the table. I'll be there in five minutes!"

Karissa got up from her bed and quickly walked to her kitchen. It was getting dark outside. She walked to the wall by the dining room and stayed behind the large table. She understood why Bolton had told her to go there. The dining room offered complete visibility in front of her and gave her protection from behind thanks to the wall.

After about five minutes, Bolton stormed into the house. "Karissa!" he yelled, looking around for her.

"Bolton, can you tell me what the hell's going on?" she said, revealing herself from behind the table.

"Yeah," Bolton said while sighing in relief. "Let's sit down." He pulled out his gun and put it on the dining room table, just in case. He made sure all of the doors and windows were locked. "The cult is targeting you and Lewis."

"What do you mean?"

"They are killing people who they believe are not allowed to live. It's way bigger than we thought, as it's spread across the country. The symbol carved into these people, it doesn't belong to any cult we're aware of, but we are learning more about them. They're being led by a man named Calvin. Anyway, that tall thing that showed up to your house that night...I hate to say it, but it easily could've killed you guys, but it didn't. The other day, when Lewis and I were in the church, that tall man could've killed Lewis but didn't. The question needs to be asked: why are they killing these other people but not Lewis?"

"Well, the tall man who came to our house could've killed me too."

"That's what I want to talk to you about, Karissa." His eyes looked down for a second before he raised them again. "You said you were supposed to come home tomorrow, right?"

She nodded in confirmation.

"Last night, Greta and Dan Armitage were murdered in their home."

Karissa lost her breath and began to tremble. Her eyes widened. Beads of sweat formed on her forehead.

"Listen, I believe they are after Lewis. They aren't killing him. However..." He paused, as he knew Karissa understood. "Listen, I'm putting you under full police protection, okay? You'll have a police car with two officers watching your house at all times."

Karissa sat there in silence. Her eyes were staring at the table in front of her. She understood what Bolton was saying. If she didn't leave Sunday morning, both she and Lisa might've been killed. She tried to breathe but couldn't.

"Karissa, I need to know something. Is there anything you can think of about your husband's life that might've been morally skewed?"

"What do you mean?"

"Okay, I need to ask these next questions. I am in no way assuming anything; I just want a little more clarity."

Karissa nodded.

"Has Lewis ever cheated on you?"

"No. He never has and never would," she replied with tears forming in her eyes. She was still in shock over Greta and Dan's deaths.

"Has he ever stolen any money, perhaps from the school?"

"No. Nothing like that."

"Has he ever killed anybody?" Bolton asked, concerned.

Then, the front door opened.

"Karissa?"

Both she and Bolton looked up.

"Lewis," Bolton said, surprised.

"What's going on here?" Lewis asked curiously.

"What's going on here? How about you answer us first!" Karissa said, turning bright red. "Where the hell were you?!" she screamed.

Bolton stood up and walked toward the door. He said, "I'll give you guys a minute."

"Karissa, you called Bolton?"

"What else was I supposed to do? My husband didn't return my calls for two days straight! Then I find out you were helping him with the investigation! Lewis, you told me you were moving on. I believed you. But no, you just had to figure it out, didn't you? Now this cult is after me too."

"Wait, what do you mean?"

"I came home early—yesterday, as I informed you in my messages. Lisa's parents were murdered in their house last night."

Lewis' mouth dropped. "Are you okay?" he asked, walking over to the table and sitting in what had been Bolton's seat.

"Lewis, I'm not going to ask again. Where the hell were you?"

"Okay, Karissa." He turned around to make sure they were alone. "You need to trust me. I'll tell you everything, but I can't tell Bolton, otherwise we're all dead—or at least, I think so."

"What?" she said, her eyes widening.

"You need to trust me." Lewis stared into her eyes.

"Okay." She calmed down a bit.

Lewis stood up and walked over to the front door. He walked out and greeted Bolton.

"Hey, Bolton," he said, putting his hands in his pockets.

"Lewis, where the hell were you?" the detective asked quietly. He was angry.

"I went for a drive in the mountains and lost my phone."

"I'm calling bullshit."

"I don't care what you call it, that's what happened."

"So, if I checked your pocket, your phone wouldn't be there?"

"Nope," Lewis said, looking off into the distance.

"Take care of your wife, Lewis."

"The hell is that supposed to mean?" Lewis said, turning bright red.

"I mean, look at her. You're seriously just abandoning her, man."

"Hey, my marriage is none of your concern, you son of a bitch. Get the hell off my property."

Bolton let out a sigh and started walking to his SUV. "This is the real deal, Lewis. Your wife is in danger. I have officers on their way to watch your house. Call me when you settle down and want to talk. I have a lot I want to tell you."

He got in his car and drove off. Lewis thought, *Yeah, I do too.* He walked back inside, and Karissa was standing up. She ran over to him and jumped into his arms. They kissed passionately.

"I'm so sorry, baby," he said, putting his hand on the side of her face.

"I'm still really mad at you," she said, getting choked up. She released a tear from her eye.

Lewis wiped it away. "I'm here. I'm here," he said while pulling her into his arms.

The tick in his brain stopped. When he was with Karissa, he was reminded of home. He loved her. As he held her in his arms, he thought to himself, *If I love her this much, why the hell did I put her through this? Why didn't I return her calls? Why the hell did I go to that stupid cabin? Why won't I tell Bolton about the letter or Reggie? I have all of the answers but...something is stopping me.*

*

That night, Lewis told Karissa everything. He told her about the cabin and the cult. The only thing he told her that wasn't the truth was that he wasn't considering leaving for Iceland.

He was definitely considering it.

He made her dinner, and they watched a movie. Afterward, they were lying in their bed. Karissa was wrapped in Lewis' arms. She made him swear that he would be completely honest from there on out. However, she still didn't tell him about his sleepwalking incidents. She knew he had enough on his plate, especially with everything he had just told her.

They locked eyes and said nothing for a while. Then Karissa suddenly spoke.

"You need to tell Bolton about what happened. Tell him everything about the cabin."

Lewis pulled away. "I can't."

"Why not?"

"If he finds out, the old man, Reggie, said that the cult would send those 'Angels.'"

"He already did, Lewis. I told you."

"Why haven't you told Lisa?" Before she could answer, he continued, "It's to protect her, right? You're letting the police tell her so you don't have to be the one to hurt her. It's the same reasoning, except instead of mentally hurting the people I'm close to, the cult will physically hurt them...including you."

Karissa thought that was a bunch of BS. She thought that the only way to stop the cult was to get the FBI involved.

Thanks to Lewis telling her everything, she knew it all too. Now she had to decide: tell Bolton and piss off her husband, or not say a word, which would keep her husband happy but allow the cult to keep killing people.

She knew what she had to do.

The only problem was, Lewis knew what she was thinking. They couldn't lie to each other. He saw the truth all over her face. That didn't worry him, however, because deep down he knew it was the right call. But something was holding him back. A certain itch in his brain told him not to. It told him to do something more drastic.

He was with Karissa, and yet he felt as though he wasn't in control of his body. It was like he was in the back seat letting someone else drive. His mind drifted off. Karissa kept calling his name. It took about four times for him to come back to reality.

"Lewis?"

"My bad," he said, shaking his head. "Long day."

He turned off the lights and began to kiss her. His lips met her neck, and she moaned softly.

He whispered, "I love you." She repeated those words back to him.

He put his hands under her shirt and began unbuttoning her bra. They laughed as the midnight sun shined brightly in the sky.

*

At around 2:00 a.m., Lewis awoke in a cold sweat. He let out a strange sound, as if he had to say "ah" at the dentist's office. The itch was stronger than it had ever been. It forced him to make strange noises he couldn't control. His eyes widened as he sprung out of bed and walked into the kitchen. He opened the refrigerator and pulled out some orange juice. He started chugging out of the bottle as if he had been stuck in the desert for a week. Juice leaked out of his mouth onto his shoulders. He put the bottle down, but he still felt thirsty.

Dripping sweat, he cursed and walked to the bathroom. Sweat poured off his head, and his skin was bright red.

Something entered his mind.

He saw images of a black church on a hill.

Of a large tree.

A cliffside.

Blood-soaked snow.

"No. No. No." He spoke to himself quietly. He dropped his head.

"Shit," he said out loud.

Quickly walking into his bedroom, Lewis opened up his laptop, which lay on the desk next to their bed. He dimmed its brightness to make sure the light wouldn't wake Karissa. He opened up the internet browser and typed in, "Flights to Iceland."

## ~ 8 ~

The following morning, Karissa woke to the sound of heavy rain pounding on her window. Before she opened her eyes, she reached over to Lewis' side of the bed. Her eyes widened when she felt nothing there.

"Lewy?" she called out, but there was no reply.

Startled, she quickly got out of bed and went to the bathroom. She noticed his toothbrush was missing. Her eyes caught something else: a small yellow sticky note was slapped to the wall where the bathroom mirror used to be. On it were two words in Lewis' handwriting:

"I'm sorry."

*

Bolton was enjoying an egg and cheese sandwich in his car. He was parked on the curb at the airport, waiting for Agent Phil, who was flying in to help with the case. A bit of melted cheese slung out of his mouth onto his black sports coat.

"Ah, damn," he mumbled around a mouthful.

His phone began to ring. He used his finger to pull the string of cheese away from his mouth and coat and answered the call.

"Hello?" Bolton said, distracted.

"Andrew, I need you."

Bolton could tell who it was, and he instantly became focused. "Karissa? What's wrong?"

"Lewis left."

"Wait, what?" he said, sitting up in his seat.

"I woke up this morning, and he was gone."

"Okay, I'm coming." He hung up the call and fastened his seat belt. He could tell she had been crying. As he peeled out of the airport, he called Phil, but there was no answer. He figured Phil was at baggage claim or something like that. He left him a message telling him to get a cab.

When Bolton arrived at the Nelsons' house, he skirted to a stop and got out. He ran to the door and opened it without knocking.

"Karissa!" he yelled.

She walked out of her bedroom wiping a tear. Bolton noticed a yellow note in her hand. He asked her what was going on.

She didn't answer.

She just handed him the note and hugged him. She began to bawl. Bolton hugged her back while he looked at the note. Anger filled up his heart. Hearing Karissa cry like that flipped a switch inside of him. He clenched his fists, crumpling the note in the process.

Bolton had had enough. Enough of Lewis. Enough of Commissioner Byrd. Enough of this cult. He was reminded of the Currys—he remembered what happened that day. He released himself from Karissa's embrace. He grabbed her by the hand and looked her in the eyes.

"Karissa, I need to know. Is there any place he could've gone?"

"Iceland..."

"What? Why Iceland?" Karissa didn't answer at first. "Karissa, why Iceland?" He raised his voice.

"That's where the cult is," she said, wiping another tear. "The night after you guys went to the church, Lewis got a note from the cult telling him to meet a man named Reggie at a cabin, and when he got there, the guy told him everything."

Bolton was shocked and upset by the news, but there was no time for anger. "Okay, where is this guy?"

"Dead. He shot himself after he told Lewis everything."

"Jesus Christ." Bolton sat there for a minute, trying to process everything. "Where in Iceland is Lewis going?"

"That, I don't know," she said with her head down.

"I need to call the bureau."

"I'm going after Lewis."

"Karissa, no. Let me handle this."

"No! I'm going after my husband!" she screamed, tears flowing down her soft face.

"It's not safe! I'm going after him!"

"Then come with me," she said. "We'll get him together. Get what you need to get, and let's go."

"Karissa, it's not—"

"That's it, Bolton! You either come with me now, or I'm going myself. It's your choice."

"Fine," he finally said after a minute of contemplation. "It's no wonder you and Lewis are married; you're both stubborn as hell."

*

Agent Phil arrived at the police station around noon, thanks to an officer who picked him up from the airport after Bolton left. When he got there, the first thing on his agenda was to talk to Byrd. He had a few questions.

Phil walked at an intimidating pace through the station until he arrived at Byrd's door. He didn't even bother to knock.

Byrd was caught off guard.

"Uh...hello?"

Phil cut him off. "Hello, sir. I'm Agent Phil from the FBI, and I wanted to ask you a few questions."

Byrd was angry, and Phil could tell. He sat down in the chair across from Byrd's desk and cleared his throat.

"With the incident regarding the death of Patrick Hopkins, I understand your department closed the case. But because of the work of Detective Bolton, you were forced to reopen it, yes?"

"That's correct." Byrd exhaled while adjusting in his seat.

"Can I ask why our very own agent who we sent over here to help tried to speak his mind but was given the cold shoulder by the commissioner in charge?"

"Listen, the investigation was open until the following day, when we eliminated the suspect. Case closed. At least, we thought it was."

"Exactly," Phil said immediately. "You thought. Because, if I'm not mistaken, Bolton continued his investigation and found that a cult with sinister intentions had been living in your city, correct?"

"Yeah, I suppose so," Byrd said, obviously irritated.

"And this abandoned chapel, how did you not think to look there, considering it's been a part of the city for a while? Were you aware of the urban legends surrounding that very chapel?"

Byrd looked down and gritted his teeth. "Those are just stories, and we wished to move on from the case, considering the suspect had been killed on the bridge."

"Everybody wished to move on from the case? Or *you* wished to move on from the case?"

Byrd rolled his eyes.

"Another thing—didn't you lose two officers during the showdown on the bridge that night? What about their families? You didn't think it was right to get justice for their murders?"

"We did. We killed the thing that killed them."

"But you couldn't see the bigger picture. I mean, Bolton said you didn't even bother to have an investigation, and you tried to stop him from even looking into anything."

"When something hideous happens in this city, it is my job to calm the citizens down and keep them safe. I thought it best to move on; we'd killed the guy. Bolton decided to get that teacher involved, and they found the abandoned church downtown."

Agent Phil didn't know about Lewis being involved, but that didn't stop his questioning. "So you didn't even get a little bit suspicious, even after the autopsy results came back ? Are you familiar with the spiral symbol that we've been finding? Are you aware that the modifications on the tall men could only have been done by somebody else?" Before Byrd could answer, Phil continued, "Because I'm sure the coroner told you his thoughts on the matter as well, right? Even he made it well aware that he thought there was something bigger. Have you spoken to the coroner, Mr. Byrd?"

Byrd let out a small sigh of annoyance. "Yes."

"Okay, so you *did* know that the first suspect's body alterations, including the absence of eyelids, the carved-up cheekbones, and even the spiral carved into his sternum, were all done by somebody else, correct?"

Byrd didn't speak.

"I'd like to know," Phil continued, "why? Given you knew all this information and had an FBI agent trying help with the investigation, which not only included the death of a citizen but the deaths of two of your officers, why would you not want the help?"

"I already told you, damn it!" Byrd's face turned bright red. "I want you out of my office! I'm sick of you feds! I'm tired of explaining myself over and over again! Get out of my town! I didn't ask for you to be here!"

Phil remained calm. "Hm, really? Because our records show that your department asked for Bolton specifically. Now, why is that? If you were just going to close the case anyway after you found the suspect, why specifically ask for an FBI agent you aren't even going to use?"

"I asked for Detective Bolton because Patrick Hopkins was mutilated. I heard of Bolton's former endeavors and figured he was the best man for the job. And once he killed the man on the bridge, I felt it was over. Even after the autopsy, and even now, after what we found at the chapel. This city needs to move on. It's over."

Agent Phil looked Byrd in the eyes and scoffed. Then he walked out of the office, slamming the door behind him. He then pulled out his phone and called Bolton.

No answer.

He called again.

Nothing.

One last time.

Bolton picked up.

"Bolton, where are you? We need to speak about Byrd. This guy is all the way off."

"I'm at the Nelsons' house."

"The teacher? What the hell are you doing there?"

"Just come over here. We can talk about everything."

"Damn it, man. I'm on my way; send me the address."

\*

As Agent Phil was driving on the cold, wet, suburban road, he saw Mount Hood peeking through the clouds as rain tapped on his window. He was going over the conversation he'd had with Byrd. He didn't want to leave any detail out when he got to the Nelsons'.

The phone rang, and without taking his eyes off the road, he told the Bluetooth in his car to answer.

"Agent Phil. This is Detective Carl. I'm stationed in Chicago. I wanted to let you know Claire Fox was found deceased earlier today."

"Damn it!" Phil's eyes filled up with anger, and a vein in his forehead began to bulge. "And the suspect?"

"Got away but was described as extremely tall."

Phil punched his steering wheel. He thanked Carl and hung up. When he came upon the Nelsons' house, he skidded to a stop and got out of his car in a hurry. He jogged to the door and knocked on it three times.

Bolton answered. Anger radiated off his face. Phil had never seen that before.

"We need to talk," the detective said in a flat voice.

Bolton led Phil inside and introduced him to Karissa, who was sitting on a brown chair in the living room, lost in thought, tearstains on her rosy cheeks. Bolton told Phil to sit down in the living room while he got everybody some coffee. Well, tea for Karissa. When they all sat down, Phil began.

"Okay, I'll start. I think Byrd is in on it."

Both Karissa and Bolton looked at him like he was crazy.

"I know, I know. But hear me out," Agent Phil continued. "The department specifically asked for you to come help with the Hopkins investigation. We weren't even interested in the damn thing because it was just another person killed on the street—nothing a police department couldn't solve. Since you're a newer agent, the director okayed the request to get you some experience."

Bolton shook off that new information, as it didn't matter now.

"However," Agent Phil began again, "when the autopsy came back and the incident on the bridge occurred, you figured there was more to this case than met the eye. You asked for his help, and he told you no even though two of his officers were killed. You went ahead and got the teacher involved, which is this young woman's husband, correct?"

They both nodded their heads.

Phil continued. "So, your lead was that it was a cult, and this 'Lewis' led you to a small, abandoned church downtown. In doing so, you both hit the jackpot and found more than enough evidence to warrant our involvement. Seems a little convenient, doesn't it? You both figured it out so easily, and he didn't. It was so obvious that a college professor who knew about the abandoned church from old urban legends figured it out, so why didn't the police commissioner even bother to check there? So, to conclude, we have a police chief unwilling to help, a missing professor, bodies turning up everywhere across the country, and also the question of why you specifically were asked for. It doesn't make much sense."

They all pondered.

"Unless it does," Karissa said quietly. "The tall man arrived at our house and only stalked us when he was killing everybody else, right? You think Byrd is in on it because he keeps trying to close the case even though there is an abundance of evidence. I think I know what's going on."

Both agents listened to the journalist intently.

"Byrd isn't just part of it. He has to be a leader of some kind. Or maybe even a scout."

Both men looked at her with wide eyes.

"Think about it," she continued. "Who knows more about the people in a city than its police commissioner? Bolton, he asked for you specifically, and now he doesn't want anything to do with you. What if he was forced to ask you here? I think you're here for a reason, and whoever told him to get you here wanted you and Lewis to search the abandoned church like you did."

"Why do you think they want me?" Bolton asked.

"Somebody needs to search his desk or his house or something, because it's obvious to me," Karissa said. She then told the story of Lewis and the cabin, and Agent Phil raised his eyebrows. She told him how Lewis was considered the chosen one. She told him how her husband had gone to Iceland, and that she was going after him.

Bolton ran his hands through his hair and said he was going with her.

Phil cleared his throat and looked at Bolton. "So, uh, when were you going to tell me this information?"

Bolton wiped some sweat off his head and said, "I just found out too."

"So, while you both go after Lewis in Iceland, I am to stay here and look through Byrd's things?"

Bolton nodded in confirmation. "You can contact the bureau and ask for backup or try to get a search. Give them all of the information we have. The more people we have working on this, the better."

"You both are going to this cult's main headquarters, and you're not taking anything? Let me call the director and see if we can give you any sort of backup."

"Okay. We're in agreement then," Karissa said, biting her lip. "Andrew and I will go to Iceland and find Lewis, while you, Phil, investigate Byrd and shut down his operation here."

"Sounds like a plan," Phil said as he shook the reporter's hand from across the table.

\*

It was another cold and brisk day in Portland. Two days had passed since her conversation with Bolton and Agent Phil, and Karissa was getting impatient. Phil had managed to get Bolton and Karissa on a private flight to Iceland, thanks to the FBI. However, a warrant for the search of the personal property of Police Commissioner John Byrd was denied.

Agent Phil decided to do it on his own, as he really didn't like the guy and thought the situation was fishy.

He took the denial of the search warrant to mean that the cult was more intertwined in the government than he thought. Especially because he'd given such good evidence and reason to search Byrd's home and office.

When the bureau was so quick to get Karissa and Bolton overseas, it pretty much confirmed that the FBI had been compromised as well. It also confirmed Karissa's theory of Bolton being a part of the cult's plan. Bolton wanted to ask the FBI a million questions when they approved the private flight, but he kept his mouth shut, as he was getting what he wanted.

They were being sent over with two handguns, a shotgun, and two other agents for backup. Their so-called mission would be off the record, however, because the FBI did not have jurisdiction in Iceland.

So, while Karissa and Bolton were packing their things to leave that night, Phil was staking out Byrd's house. He was sitting in a black Camaro with tinted windows a block down the street. The house was in his view.

It was a nice suburban home with big windows. The fog, however, got worse and worse throughout the day, causing Phil to have to get closer and closer. His plan was to break in to Byrd's house under the cover of night and look around for any confirmation he was working with the cult. He knew Byrd worked constantly and didn't come home until late, thanks to some scouting the previous two days.

By 2:00 p.m., the fog was so dense nobody could've seen five feet in front of them. Phil decided to use this to his advantage and go in. He picked up a backpack from his passenger seat and reached inside. He pulled out a Beretta M9 pistol and checked to make sure it was loaded. He then slid the clip into the gun and put it in his holster.

He stepped out of the car and pulled a mask up over his mouth and nose. He was in all-black clothing and needed to disguise himself since this was completely illegal. As he started walking up to the house, he noticed that, sure enough, there was no car in the driveway.

He was clear to enter.

Phil walked around back and checked to see if the door was locked. It was. Phil hadn't thought it would be *that* easy, but he had a motto: "You always gotta check."

He pulled out a small knife and used it to pick the lock. Once he heard a *click*, he knew it was open.

When he walked in, nothing seemed out of the ordinary. Phil walked through the kitchen and the living room.

Nothing.

Next, the bathroom and bedrooms.

Nothing.

He went upstairs and checked all the rooms up there.

Again, nothing.

There was one more room off to the right side of the hallway. When he walked in, he realized it was Byrd's bedroom. He could tell because the bed had not been made, and there were clothes on the floor, while the other bedrooms looked like they'd been set up for an open house.

At first glance, there was nothing out of the ordinary. Phil kept looking around.

Still nothing.

He saw a few pictures on Byrd's dresser and examined them more closely. The first was of a woman. Phil didn't know Byrd was married. Maybe it was his sister or something? The next photo was of Byrd and another man. The man was skinny and bald. He was wearing all black. There was something off about the guy, and it gave Phil the chills.

He kept looking around and noticed a door that led to Byrd's closet. When he walked in, he noticed a square hatch with a rope hanging from the ceiling. It clearly led to the attic. He proceeded to open the door, and a ladder dropped down.

Phil climbed it and entered the attic. When he got to the top, he looked around and saw a whole bunch of boxes. They were all very neat, and none of them had even a single dust particle on them.

Phil also noticed that every single box was black and had a cover over it. He decided to open some boxes and see what was inside. The first one he opened was not too big and not too small.

Inside was a black robe. He looked underneath it and noticed another piece of black cloth. He pulled it out of the box, revealing a large, black, pointy hood with two eyeholes.

"Holy shit," Phil said quietly.

Something else caught his eye. He folded the hood and robe back into the box and put it right back where it was. He walked past the clutter of boxes and toward the color red.

When he was finally close enough to realize what he was looking at, his mouth dropped. It was a bright red robe over a mannequin. It had a tall, pointy hood the matched the robe. In the middle of the hood, right above the eyeholes, there was a black spiral. There were a number of patches on the robe, although Phil had no idea what they meant.

He pulled out his phone and started taking pictures of the red robe and the black boxes.

*Karissa was right—Byrd isn't just a part of this, he's a MAJOR part of it*, he thought to himself.

He walked up to the red robe and noticed a red leather notebook with a black spiral engraved on it. He opened it up and began to read. The first few pages were photos of a large black church. The next page featured a photo of a man standing on an altar, preaching to a crowd of people in black cloaks. However, they were not angels.

They were normal people.

Phil skipped a few pages until he saw a word that caught his eye: "Andrew."

Phil flipped back and noticed the name Andrew Bolton. He began to read.

*The detective has become a nuisance. I don't know what Calvin sees in him. Word has gotten to me that Reginald has told Lewis about us. It is almost time. Everything is going to plan. However, I do not think that Andrew should be Lewis' Angel. I personally believe that it should be his wife, Karissa. I know that no angel has been a woman, but their bond may make them unstoppable, and we are entering an era that none of us—including Calvin—have been a part of. He wishes to throw away the bond and have Karissa killed; he thinks it will be the spark that lights Artemis in Lewis. I think it will be much of a waste.*

Phil's eyes widened with fear and shock. He was preparing to take a picture of that page, but a loud noise from downstairs stopped him in his tracks. Instead of taking pictures, he grabbed the book and put it in his jacket pocket, then quickly and quietly walked over to the attic door and closed it from the inside.

He heard footsteps.

Except they were not regular footsteps. They sounded big and lazy.

He sat there in absolute silence and listened intently. The steps got louder and louder. He could then hear another set of footsteps. These were also big and heavy. It was as if each step shook the house. After a few moments, the footsteps got louder and louder, until he knew that whoever it was, was in Byrd's room.

He then heard the closet door open.

Phil knew he had to move. He took one step, and the floor beneath him creaked loudly.

Phil froze, and the footsteps stopped.

It was quiet for a long moment.

Then, all of a sudden, a huge hand broke through the bottom of the attic and grabbed Phil's ankle. The assailant pulled him down through the floor with a great crash. Dust filled the air as pieces of the ceiling fell around him.

Phil let out a groan, then looked up to find two extremely tall figures, both in black robes and black pointy hoods. They were both easily over seven feet tall, and the hood added another foot... Angels. Everyone was still for a moment, until Phil decided to make the first move and pull out his pistol. He aimed it at them from the floor, but right before he could pull the trigger, one of the Angels swiped the gun away with great force.

Phil watched the gun fly out of Byrd's room toward the stairs. He looked back and saw both beings making their way toward him. He was now fully realizing his situation. He tried to get up and run, but one of the Angels grabbed him by the throat.

Phil pulled out the knife he had in his back pocket and jabbed it into the neck of the robed figure who held him in his grasp. Blood spewed from its jugular, and the Angel dropped the agent. Phil hit the ground and immediately took off for the bedroom door, but before he could reach it, a long arm stretched out and clotheslined him, knocking Phil down hard on his back.

The other tall being stood there and looked down at Phil, who was groaning as if he'd run straight into a brick wall. Then Phil looked into the hallway and saw his gun.

The Angel tilted his head in confusion as Phil rolled out of the room. But before he could get to his gun, the Angel grabbed him by the shirt collar, lifted him up, and threw him down the stairs. Phil's foot thankfully swept the gun down the stairs with him. His head, however, hit the railing and broke it, slicing his skull open. He crashed into the kitchen counter, causing it to break.

Phil looked up and saw the Angel standing at the top of the stairs. It wasn't in a hurry. It just lazily shuffled down, step by step, its massive hood still on.

It wasn't a moment later before the other Angel walked out of the room. Blood was still spurting from its neck. Its hood was off, and Phil finally got a look at the face of an Angel. The wide, bulging eyes that could never shut. The smile that was permanently there. The hideous gray color of his skin and the yellowish orange drool that dripped from his mouth. It stood there as if it had not been stabbed in the neck just two minutes ago.

Phil sat there in disbelief.

"Goddamn it," he said, lowering his head, noticing there wasn't much he could do.

The undamaged Angel took another slow step down the staircase.

Phil tried to get up, but his body was broken. He pulled his mask off and noticed it was stained with blood. The blood from his head began to enter his eye as it streamed down his face. He sighed, knowing what was about to happen. After he finished examining his mask and essentially calling it quits, he threw it off to the side.

As he did, he noticed his pistol was nearby. His eyes widened as he realized he may still have a chance. Phil quickly worked up the gumption to move, but an immense amount of pain stopped him. He looked down and noticed he had a piece of the wooden staircase stuck in his thigh. He was bleeding from that wound, too, and he could barely move. His injuries wouldn't allow it.

He felt his shattered ribs, his slashed face, his impaled thigh, and all the other injuries that couldn't be classified yet. They were holding him back. The tall beings slowly walked past the halfway point of the staircase as Phil put all of his energy into his next move. He screamed loudly and flipped his body over, allowing him to crawl to the gun. He reached out and grabbed it.

He quickly aimed it at the Angels, who were now at the bottom of the stairs. Phil mumbled softly, "Come on, you bastards."

He shot three times into the chest of the first one. The Angel stopped for a moment but continued to walk toward him. Phil widened his eyes. "Oh, you gotta be fucking kidding me!"

Phil kept crawling toward the back door from which he'd entered. He thought about his options. His clip held twelve bullets, and three were gone. He thought about unloading the clip into one of them, but he realized that every bullet counted. If he used all the bullets on just one of them, the other would still be after him.

He couldn't finish his thinking, as the first Angel leaned down, grabbed Phil by the ankle, and began to pull him closer. Phil reacted by putting the gun right in front of the Angel's face and pulling the trigger. Blood and brains exploded out of the back of its head as it dropped to the floor.

Dead.

Phil realized: headshots.

He aimed the pistol at the next one's head, and he shot three times. The other Angel dropped to the floor in a pool of blood.

Phil lay there still. He let out a loud scream of victory. Then he heard police sirens in the distance.

*

Lewis awoke from his dream to find himself on the plane he'd boarded the night before. He realized how upset Karissa was going to be when she woke up, and for good reason. He thought back to Bolton's words when he'd told him that he needed to take better care of his wife. Lewis knew he was right.

*Why am I doing this?* he thought.

He knew that if he'd just stayed with Karissa that night, he would have been fine. But now he was on a journey that could possibly lead to his death, or even something worse. He saw what the Angels looked like; he'd met with Reggie in the cabin, who told him that he was needed and then proceeded to shoot himself in the head. There was no logical reason for Lewis to be going to Iceland, and he knew it.

As soon as he started thinking about turning back, he felt a spasm in the back of his neck. He began to sweat. His hands started to shake, and his face started twitching.

The man sitting next to him stopped watching his movie and asked the professor if he was all right. Lewis yelled out, "I'm fine!" and suddenly a wave of darkness fell over him.

He passed out.

When Lewis awoke a few minutes later, he was surprised to see a flight attendant in front of him, asking if he was okay.

"Yeah, I'm fine, I have narcolepsy," he said, trying to come up with something fast.

The flight attendant said, "Okay." She gave him a cup of water. Lewis thanked her, and as she walked away, the intercom turned on, and the pilot's voice announced that they would be landing soon.

When Lewis exited the plane, he noticed it was a small airport. He hadn't brought anything other than a backpack filled with an extra set of clothes. He was wearing a black flannel underneath his leather jacket and had on dark blue jeans and combat boots. His brown hair, now in long strands, fluttered in the crisp air.

Dalvik was cold. Much colder than Portland. The sun was out, but there was a large wall of dark clouds over the horizon. Lewis looked around and decided to walk into town. The village was colorful, each building painted in bright reds, blues, and yellows. The smell of fish ran through his nostrils, and the sound of boats in the harbor rang in his ears.

He had no idea where to go, so he figured he would just explore. After a few moments, he saw out of the corner of his eye two women standing behind a small building. They were wearing black clothing and staring at him with wide eyes, as if they knew him.

Lewis put his head down and decided to keep walking. However, the itch in his neck grew stronger with every step that he took away from the women. He kept walking, but the itch turned into a pain like a migraine. The pain became so intense that Lewis started groaning and grinding his teeth. He even started drooling out of the corner of his mouth.

He'd finally had enough, so he turned toward the ladies, and the pain suddenly faded. He saw the women laugh.

"What the hell, man," Lewis said to himself, stunned by what had just happened. He figured he had no choice but to start walking toward the women.

They never took their eyes off of him. One of them even started twisting the ends of her blonde hair.

"Hello," he said nervously, followed by a small wave of his hand as he arrived.

One of the women, who was quite beautiful, grabbed his hand and said, "Come."

She led him to a truck behind a small building. There was a man sitting in the driver's seat. He was bald and wearing black robes. The pretty woman who led Lewis had him climb in the back of the truck, and she climbed in after him.

Once they were seated, she looked at the other woman, who was still standing by the truck. They both made a fist, put it to their chest, and let out a noise that sounded like a gasp for air. It was quick but terrifying, and it threw Lewis completely off.

The one who was standing then disappeared behind the building as the truck started up and they began to drive away. Lewis, still extremely nervous, was looking around awkwardly, trying not to make eye contact, but the woman just kept staring.

He finally met her gaze.

"What?" Lewis asked.

The woman laughed playfully in return.

It was extremely windy in the back of the truck. Lewis began to shake because he was so cold. He looked at the woman again and asked if she was cold.

She replied with another playful laugh and smile.

They drove for about thirty minutes before the truck slowed down and pulled off onto a dirt road. Lewis' anxiety began to rise. He looked up and tried to see where the road led, but the wall of gray clouds had made its way to the area, causing snowflakes to begin their descent from the heavens, making it hard to see too far in front of them. He did notice, though, that the dirt road went on for a while and led to the top of a hill.

They were definitely at high elevation—possibly in the mountains, but Lewis couldn't see.

"Where are we going?" Lewis said while still looking at the road.

"Calvin," the woman said as she grabbed his ice-cold hand.

Lewis pulled away fast and sat back down. The woman tried to grab his hand again, but the professor pulled it away.

"Uh, no, thank you," Lewis said, smiling nervously.

The woman's face twisted into a pout, and she let out a sad noise. Lewis slowly turned his head away to watch the road again.

They started their ascent up the hill.

Lewis noticed a cluster of buildings surrounded by a wall, although the fog and snow didn't allow much visibility. They kept getting closer until Lewis was able to see what looked like a village.

Tall, dark gates made from wood and stone stood in their path.

The truck came to a stop. Two tall Angels in all-black robes with long, pointed hoods were guarding a gate. This was the first time Lewis had seen them with something covering their faces, but that didn't stop him from feeling extremely uneasy.

He knew what was under those hoods, and the way they made them seem about a foot taller than they already were sent a thousand chills up Lewis' spine.

Both of the Angels were holding spears. One of them moved its hand slightly, and the gates opened, revealing a black-and-red sign that read, "Blackgate."

The first thing that met Lewis' eyes were the hundreds of people dressed in all-black robes. They were standing on either side of the truck, which began to drive through the village. They all began to clap as they looked at Lewis. The woman in the bed of the truck with him began to clap as well.

Lewis looked up and noticed a very large and tall black church that stood at the end of the road on top of a hill. The rows of people lined the road all the way up its front doors. Once the truck got to the church, it stopped, and the woman jumped out of the back with a big smile on her face. She grabbed Lewis' hand and said, "Come!"

Lewis, not pulling his hand away this time, hopped out the back. When he got down, she kissed him on the cheek and ran away laughing. Then she faded into the crowd of people.

There were so many thoughts going through his head, and he barely had time to take everything in, because all of a sudden, the big doors of the church opened up with a loud creak, and everybody stopped clapping.

They all got down on one knee, put their fists over their chests, and bowed their heads. A man led by two Angels in black robes and pointy hoods walked out. The man was tall, about six foot three, and he was as bald as a watermelon. He was in a cherry red robe and wore large rings on his fingers. His face featured a massive scar down one cheek.

He approached Lewis and looked at him with a smile.

"My son," he said softly. "Our future has arrived!" he said loudly.

The crowd of people cheered as the man grabbed Lewis by the shoulder and led him into the church. The Angels followed and shut the doors behind them. As soon as the doors shut, the cheers immediately stopped, which added another thought to the overwhelming barrage that was already on Lewis' mind.

Inside the church, Lewis noticed a large Nordic rune that sat above the altar. The stained-glass windows were all red and featured a black spiral or another rune on them. It was dark inside. There were seven other men with red robes and pointy hoods standing by the altar.

"You must have a million questions," the bald man said to Lewis. And with a wave of his hand, all the men in red robes exited the church. The only people left inside were this strange man, Lewis, and two Angels standing by the large church doors.

"Please, sit," the man said as he gestured toward the first row of pews. The bald man sat down on the stairs that led to the altar, so they were facing each other.

"First and foremost, let me introduce myself. My name is Calvin Roche. The folks around here, however, know me as the Father of Artemis."

Lewis just sat there, looking at Calvin blankly. He spoke softly, normally. But there was definitely something off about him. Lewis just couldn't tell what.

"Well," Calvin continued, "I have done a great deal to get you here, Lewis. A great deal, indeed."

"How long have you been doing this?" Lewis finally asked.

"Well, you see, every hundred years, Artemis finds a new Father. Somebody to lead the followers to their purpose until we find the chosen one. Once we do that, we can finally do what our King requires and perform the final ritual; the Cleansing."

"Wait, you're a hundred years old?"

"Why, yes, I am," Calvin said, chuckling. "Things work differently here. We have a book that describes our whole existence and the rules we need to abide by in order to please Artemis. The mighty Herja. It also features an immense number of runes and spells for things like prolonging death and enhancing our people, turning them into our lovely, lovely Angels."

Lewis sat there stunned. He couldn't believe this was actually happening.

"Okay, I'm going to need you to explain everything to me, because I don't know what the hell is going on here," Lewis said.

"Ah, yes. I am aware that receiving this information all at once can be quite daunting." Calvin then cleared his throat. "Lewis, let's start from the beginning, shall we? We are the Angels of Artemis. Reggie told you about that, correct?"

Lewis nodded.

"Good. We are here to carry out the will of our King. Artemis demands that we cleanse this world of its toxicity and horrors so that when he returns, the world is as he envisioned it when he left us so many lifetimes ago."

Calvin paused to make sure Lewis was following along. Once Lewis nodded in confirmation, he continued.

"We've been doing this for thousands of years. Everyone here has a job. When that job is completed, they will cleanse themselves, as you saw with Reggie. Most of us stay here and pray to Artemis and make lives for ourselves, as we are the chosen souls, the ones who get to live freely as long as they follow the rules in the Herja that Artemis himself wrote down. The families we have here are almost all born into this, and they stay here forever until they die. They raise their children, teach them the ways, and so on and so forth."

He paused for a quick moment to lick his lips.

"The ones who go out and complete the harder tasks, they are known as our Angels. I understand you've met some of them before. Well, Angels are chosen due to their history. They are not born into this life. They are either taken, or they stumble upon our teachings and wish to learn. Then we modify them with what we call the Dokkur Vefur. The process is extremely painful, not only to the physical body but also the mind. We chose candidates whose pasts have an overbearing weight on them, those whose minds are only held together by a string that connects reality and insanity."

"My god," Lewis said quietly.

"You see," Calvin continued, "we have embedded Angels everywhere in the world, and that one fateful night, one stumbled upon you. Why you were not cleansed was an insane shock to me because of your past, but it showed that you have a deeper meaning. And, boy oh boy, do you."

"What do you mean?" Lewis asked, feeling the nervous bile grumbling in his gut.

"Well, now you're here. It is what Artemis demands. The ones who are not modified, like your police commissioner, are there to gain information on who should be cleansed and who shouldn't be then reports back to us here. We perform our rituals and speak to Artemis and he gives the final word on if that person should be cleansed or not."

"Like Patrick Hopkins?" Lewis said with an angry look. "What did he do to deserve that?"

"Nothing that I care about," Calvin said while shrugging his shoulders. "But Artemis demanded it."

"Artemis demanded it? Okay, so then where is he?" Lewis asked, agitated.

"He is living between the line of life and death. Now he is closer than ever to return—"

Lewis cut him off. "So you told the Angels to kill Patrick and everybody else they've killed?"

"Heavens no, Lewis!" Calvin said, laughing. "We cannot communicate with the Angels. When they are modified, a special rune is carved onto them that allows Artemis to speak from the afterlife and give them commands."

Lewis sat there in disbelief.

"You see, Lewis, we are here to make the world a better place. When Artemis tells us to cleanse someone, we do it. We've been doing it for years, hiding in the shadows, as our operation has never been big enough to conquer. However, when you came along, we ran into some...issues."

"What do you mean?"

"For thousands of years, nobody knew about us except for, well, us. Sure, there were legends that people created when they saw our Angels. Like the Wendigo or Bigfoot. However, they were so far off that we didn't very much care. Now, with you and Detective Bolton involved, we've been struggling to keep us a secret."

"Wait, what does Bolton have to do with this?"

"Well, every leader in our family needs his Angels. And with you having a bigger role than any of us, it is only right that you receive the best Angel we could find. Andrew is to be yours, as his history makes it hard for his mind to stay intact. It was tough for him to start his family because he feared he would lose them, like what happened in the town that was massacred that day when he was but a boy. That one fateful day that sent him down this path. His destiny."

"You're going to capture Bolton and bring him over here to become my... Angel?"

"Only half correct, Lewis. He is coming over here by his own free will right now—with your wife, I should add."

Lewis stood up fast and slammed his hands on the pew. The Angels behind him, by the door, got into attack position. Lewis noticed but didn't care.

"YOU LEAVE HER OUT OF THIS!" Lewis screamed.

Calvin waved the Angels off, and they went back to their standing selves.

"You know the itch that you've been feeling, Lewis? That is Artemis guiding you. We've all felt it. If you don't follow the itch, it will become something you cannot live with. Nobody has ever been able to ignore Artemis, as he is the true King of the world. That will happen to you, my son. You will not be able to ignore what you must do."

"I swear to god, I will burn this place to the ground if you lay a goddamn finger on her."

"We'll see what Artemis commands, Lewis," Calvin said with a disgusting smirk. "Now come, I have more to show you."

Lewis stood up and followed Calvin through the backside of the church. The back door revealed a small graveyard with tombstones that were in almost perfect condition. The snow was falling heavier now. Calvin led Lewis through the cemetery on a cobblestone pathway. It looked as though the path led to a cliff. Lewis was worried Calvin might throw him off for some sacrifice, but he remembered how "the Father" told him he was important for "the Cleansing."

His anger built up inside of him. This man had threatened Karissa, and Lewis was still following him through some creepy pathway.

*Why?*

Sure enough, the path led to the edge of a cliff. It was overlooking the sea, and it would've been a good view if there wasn't a large shrine sitting right in front of them. The shrine was made out of stone and surrounded by leaves and other offerings. As Lewis looked closer, he saw the shrine had some stone bowls that lay on its base. They were filled with blood and what looked like fingers and toes.

"This is where Artemis was defiled by those he believed were his family," Calvin said with a smile. He lifted his hand up—the middle finger of his left hand was missing. "When you join us, you must make an offering to Artemis. It is time."

"No, no. I'm not cutting off my finger, sorry," Lewis said, chuckling nervously.

"I don't believe you have a choice," Calvin replied, and with a wave of his hand, two Angels appeared out of nowhere and knocked Lewis to the snowy ground. They pinned him there until one of them pulled out a large, rusty knife. Lewis screamed and begged for them to stop.

And with one single hack from the angel, Lewis' finger dropped into a bowl. Blood squirted out onto the base of the Artemis shrine, melting the freshly fallen snow. Lewis screamed loudly.

"Blessed be our new brother, son, father, and King," Calvin began. "Artemis shall rule once again!" The Angels let Lewis go. They put their fists to their chests and let out otherworldly groans.

Lewis sat there for a second, reeling from the pain. The words had just registered in his mind. He looked up at Calvin from the snowy ground.

"Wait, did you just call me a King?" he asked intently.

"Why, yes, Lewis. Oh, did I forget to mention? Artemis' soul is returning to this world, yes, but he needs a physical form in order to do so."

"Wait. What does that mean?" Lewis asked, groaning.

"Lewis, you will become Artemis," Calvin said with a large smile.

*

That night, Lewis was treated like a king. The second they got back from the shrine, Calvin gave Lewis a white robe to change into. He was the guest of honor, and Calvin wanted everyone to know it. A few old women helped Lewis with his now-missing finger.

Afterward, they feasted in a large dining hall type building in the village. They served meat, vegetables, ale, and fruit, and after that a platter of different kinds of cakes and desserts.

As Lewis sat there, he realized he wasn't himself. It was like somebody else was in control of his body, and he was tied down in the back seat.

He didn't want this.

He wanted Karissa.

He wanted to be back home, but he had dug himself into such a large hole that he didn't think he'd be able to get out. Calvin snapped him out of his trance and quieted down the feast by pounding on the wooden table.

"Children of Artemis!" he began. "Tonight we celebrate the arrival of our chosen one. Lewis Nelson will be the one who brings Artemis back to the land of the living. To reward him for his sacrifice, Lewis will have the pick of any sister he chooses to bed!" A few women and girls laughed and giggled.

Lewis didn't want this. All he could think about was his beautiful wife and the life they had before all of this nonsense.

*I'm done playing this charade*, he thought to himself.

He stood up.

"Uh, yeah, Calvin? I'm going to have to—" Then the pain in the base of his skull returned. His spine contorted and twisted, and his head slammed against the table, causing forks and knives to hit the floor. Then he immediately stood up with a blank expression while blood poured from his nose.

"Never mind," he said soullessly.

He smiled and walked over to the women. The girl who drove up to Blackgate with him in the truck grabbed his hand and led him outside of the dining hall. Another two young women followed. As they left, everybody else cheered loudly.

When they got outside, they had to shuffle through a bit of snow, as almost five inches had fallen now. The village was just barely lit up by the lanterns outside of each building and house.

Lewis' eyes widened. He was himself now. He realized what was happening.

"Wait, stop, please," he said sadly. Nobody could hear him. He was far away from home. From any allies. From Karissa. The pain in his neck shot through his shoulder in a jolting motion.

"Goddamn it, stop, please!" he screamed as he hit the cold ground. His body began to contort. He wasn't going to betray Karissa without a fight. His arms started bending backward. His neck twisted. He screamed louder and louder.

The girls just stood there and laughed.

The pain was so unbearable that Lewis threw up. He was losing. In his mind, he saw darkness. Pain and suffering. He saw what looked to be Vikings, being tortured and killed in hideous ways. He heard a terrifying voice. It sounded like a volcano erupting in his mind.

"Relax, I am in control now. There is no need to waste your time. I am returning to this world. They will celebrate my arrival. This world will run red with my revenge."

The vision in his mind continued. Now he saw a strong Viking king. Ruthless. Terrifying. Making sacrifices. Killing women and children during raids. Then, images of sadness from the village. No food. No resources. Then the king being led onto a cliff by his own family. Being stabbed. Dying.

The king was then on his knees, staring up at those he trusted and loved. His back was to the cliff. After a moment, a woman stepped forward and put her foot on his chest. Then she extended her leg, pushing the king off the cliff.

Then the end. He saw the king. He was face-to-face with him. His eyes were glowing red, and he was surrounded by fire. He had a helmet with horns that reached far above his head. He wore a long flowing cloak, and his legs were that of a goat.

He was a demon.

He was Artemis.

"Lewis," Artemis said, his voice low and evil. "It is pointless of you to keep fighting me. I am a god. I will return to this world and destroy those who are unworthy and flawed like I should've done so long ago."

Lewis looked at him in fear. He was terrified. He didn't think he would be able to make it out. To fight. He thought this was the end.

But then he closed his eyes. Lewis thought of that night at the party. The night he met Karissa. He thought about brushing her hair behind her ear. He thought about finding love and never letting it go. He thought of this cult and the way it had terrorized her. Threatened her. It had come to his home and attacked his family. The only person he'd ever loved.

He wasn't going to let that happen. Lewis looked up into Artemis' glowing red eyes.

"Fuck you," he said strongly.

Lewis came to on the snow. He stood up as if nothing had happened and followed the girls. They laughed and danced in the snow. Then they entered a home, and one of them began to undress immediately. Lewis smiled and kept going into the bedroom.

As they entered, one of the girls, who was too excited, hit a dresser and knocked a few things over. Lewis noticed. The girls stopped and pulled the white robe off of him. They began touching his body. All three of them went to their knees. Lewis looked at the dresser and noticed a pair of scissors. He looked down to make sure the girls were distracted.

Then he quickly grabbed the scissors and kicked one of the girls with a massive force. The other two jumped up immediately, shocked. Lewis wasted no time before he shoved the pair of scissors into another girl's neck, spewing blood. The girl from the truck ride was the last one standing. She jumped on Lewis and screamed wildly, knocking him to the floor. She began to scratch him, and her nails cut through his skin.

He kept trying to block her, but he just kept getting cut savagely. He looked around and noticed an old barber's razor on the ground. He took a scratch to the face, and that sent him over the edge. His anger gave him a second boost of energy as he reached up and grabbed her by her hair. He grabbed the razor with the other hand, pulled her head back, and cut her throat, causing her scream to transform into a gurgle, and then to silence. He got up. The girl he'd kicked was still unconscious. He held on to the razor and stared at her, thinking of what to do next.

But before he could make any decision, Lewis noticed lanterns coming his way through the fogged-up window. Calvin and the other villagers had heard the commotion and come outside the dining hall. Lewis grabbed his robe and ran out the back door. He looked around for a path and noticed a woodcutter's axe stuck in a log. He pulled it out with a huff and began to run into the cold, dark night, his pursuers hot on his tail.

\*

Bolton and Karissa arrived at the airport hangar in Portland. They stepped out of Bolton's car and grabbed their bags, which included the guns. They were then greeted by two very big FBI agents. They were both bald and wore sunglasses, and one of them had a very full beard.

Bolton greeted the agents before introducing Karissa. The one with the beard was named Agent Gray, and the other was Agent Brock. They seemed very nice, but both Karissa's and Bolton's radars were up. They knew they couldn't trust anybody. Karissa didn't want to admit it, but a small part of her didn't trust Bolton either.

She kept asking herself, *Why was Bolton asked here? What is his reason for being involved?* She also knew she had no other choice but to trust him and only him in order to get her husband back.

When they got on the plane, Agent Brock headed toward the cockpit to say something to the pilot. Karissa caught a brief glimpse inside while she was boarding. She saw that there were two pilots in there. Her initial thought was, *We're outnumbered.* They all sat down. Both of the agents went to the back of the plane, while Bolton and Karissa sat across from each other toward the front. Bolton could tell she was nervous and maybe a little scared. He grabbed her hand. She looked up at him in surprise.

"Hey," he said, looking into her eyes. "It's going to be okay. I promise. We'll find him."

She smiled back and nodded. He let go of her hand and leaned back. They were quiet until Agent Brock stood up and walked over to them.

"Y'all ready to take off?"

Both of them shook their heads, but after a short while, the plane began to move. Brock returned to his seat, and the plane took off on its way to Dalvik, Iceland.

"So," Karissa began, "did you always want to be an FBI agent?"

"No," Bolton said. "I, uh, grew up in a small town in Montana, and there were a lot of bad people. One family in particular. They tore up the town, killed people—my parents. I killed the man who did it and became a cop. Long story short, I joined the FBI because it seemed to be the only thing that I'd be good at in this world. Now I realize that's not even true."

Karissa looked at him with sympathy. "I'm so sorry. And what do you mean? You've helped us so much."

"Karissa, I needed help from your husband to solve a case. Don't get me wrong, I'm grateful for it, because he's a smart guy. But I've always done this alone, and without him

I wouldn't have gotten anywhere. But now, because I let him help, he's god knows where, and it's my fault."

"No, Andrew, it's not your fault. My husband is stubborn as hell. When he puts his mind to something, he doesn't stop until it's done. If you didn't let him help, he would've tried to do this alone, and that could've been worse. Trust me."

"I appreciate that, Karissa," Bolton said with kind eyes. "What made you want to become a reporter?"

"Well, I've always had this overbearing desire to help people. Maybe it was imprinted on me because of all the late nights I would help out my drunk friends with their problems, but it became a passion of mine. Seeing somebody broken and being able to offer them the help they need to become whole again really makes my heart happy. Being a reporter gives me that same feeling."

"Wow, that's amazing," he replied, running his hand through his blonde hair.

"Do you have a family, Detective?" Karissa asked while adjusting the ring on her finger.

"Yes, I do," Bolton said, nodding his head. "Two little girls and a loving wife."

"That's adorable. How did you guys meet?"

"Honestly, by fate," he said, laughing. "Being in this job, I don't really have too much of a social life. Hell, I barely have time for my family right now. Imagine trying to make a girl fall in love with you."

Karissa laughed as he continued.

"One time, when I worked for the sheriff's office in Casper, I had a domestic violence call at a motel. When I got there, it was a party, and the dispute was over a beer pong game. However, the suspects were passed out when I got there, and so I just checked to make sure everyone was okay. As I was leaving, I saw this one girl staring at me from the kitchen. She had these big, beautiful eyes, and I couldn't stop looking into them. It was like I was in a trance. Then, before I knew it, she was writing her number down on my notepad, and we hit it off."

Karissa said, "Aw, that's amazing."

Bolton smiled and looked out the plane window. "I promised my little girls that I'd build them a treehouse when I got home. It's something I wanted to do for them before they were born. Now one's four and the other is five, and it's still not done. I swear, this job is not as good as I used to think it was."

"Well," Karissa started, "I think when we work, especially when it's a passion, we tend to focus more on that and lose the importance of life itself. Sometimes we have to remind ourselves that we are here to live our lives. Work is work, sure, but when it becomes your life, that's when you start to see the time fade."

Bolton sighed, as he knew she was right. Once this whole endeavor was over, he was going to become a changed man. He was going to build that treehouse for his girls

He looked into Karissa's eyes. "We will find Lewis and bring him home. I promise you."

\*

Agent Phil was sitting in his hospital bed on his laptop, filing a report on the altercation at Byrd's house. It was a miracle that he was as well as he was. He only had some cracked ribs and needed stitches on his forehead, as well as the removing the piece of railing in his thigh.

He mumbled some insults under his breath, then heard a quick knock on the door. It was another FBI agent. He was tall and thin and had gray slicked-back hair. However, he was not old.

Phil sat up in his bed. "Oh, thank god. Finally!"

"Phil, you have no idea how much trouble you have gotten yourself in," the agent said.

"Bobby, you'll never believe the shit I've found, how much of this has been swept under the rug."

"You heard what I just said, right? You entered a man's home with no warrant."

"Yeah, then proceeded to find out he's part of a cult that's been killing people for years, one that's deeply embedded in our society and government. And on top of that, we have two tall jack-o'-lantern-looking bastards who attacked me. Considering what I've found, if anybody is in trouble, it's this cult."

Agent Bobby just shook his head and sat down.

"Look," Phil continued, "I've been looking all over. There are tons of cases that feature actual spirals on victims who were not just murdered, but brutally mutilated. The victims include people from crooked lawyers to unfaithful partners. People who have not been very honest or morally correct, right? Well, check this out. We haven't heard about any of this because the towns and cities where this is happening are run by people who are in the cult."

"How do you even know that, Phil?" Bobby said, shaking his head.

Phil looked around and pulled out a book with a spiral on it. Byrd's book. Bobby looked shocked.

"I pulled this from the house. Inside is a list of police officers, county and city commissioners, politicians, mailmen, journalists, and even agents of ours who are a part of this thing. Over two thousand corrupt sons of bitches!"

"Why the hell do you have it?"

"Because I'm not letting this book get into the wrong hands. I'm only showing you because your name wasn't in it."

Bobby shook his head in amazement and said, "All right, well, I was here for disciplinary reasons, but I don't think that matters now. What do you need from me?"

"We are going to take down this cult without them even knowing. It's time to cut the head off the snake."

*

Lewis ran as fast as he could. He was sluggish and stumbling due to his feet beginning to freeze in the high snow. He tripped and fell into a snowbank, causing the rest of his lightly clothed body to freeze as well.

He laid there still and held on to the axe, ready for anything. The orange glow of torches lit up the dark and snow-covered forest like a ball of fire that was coming right toward him. He crawled a bit until he got behind a tree.

He was so quiet. He knew that any sort of sound could get him killed.

He wanted to listen to what the people were saying, but it was silent. Nothing. Only the sound of the snow crunching under feet. Lewis saw the glow of the torches to his right and turned left, ready to run.

But before he could take off, he was shocked by the glow of torches there too. He crept around the tree and saw the mob had split into groups. He was afraid, unaware of what to do. He then realized it would be better to be ahead of the people than behind them. Being behind meant he only had one way to go—back to Blackgate. And who knew how many angry villagers were waiting for him there.

Going ahead of them meant he could try to outrun them. Best-case scenario, he would get back to town. Worst-case scenario, he'd end up lost in the cold and bitter Icelandic wilderness, dead from hypothermia. Either way, he had to make a decision, as he knew his tracks would soon be found.

Lewis held on to the axe and let out a deep breath to prepare. He stood up slowly, looked straight ahead, and began to sprint.

Faster than he had ever run in his entire life.

He knew breathing in the frigid air was extremely hard on his lungs, but he didn't care.

Faster. Faster.

No looking back. Just straight ahead.

*BAM!!*

Lewis was clotheslined, and he flipped and hit the ground hard. He let out a groan of pain but opened his eyes quickly. He saw a large, bald man standing in front of him holding a large shovel. He wasn't an Angel, just a regular citizen from the town.

The man said nothing and smiled.

Lewis felt around for the axe in the surrounding snow without taking his eyes off the man, who kept getting closer and closer.

The professor felt and grabbed the handle of the axe. The man, now standing over Lewis, lifted his shovel above his head, readying a potentially fatal blow.

Lewis moved faster.

He swung the axe with one hand directly into the side of the man's skull, instantly killing him. He stood up fast, realizing the Angels and rest of the search party could have heard the commotion and that he didn't have much time.

Lewis attempted to pull the axe out of the man's skull, but it was too deep, and there wasn't enough time to remove it. He turned away and ran fast. He exited the tree line and saw nothing but snow. In fact, the snow began to fall so hard that Lewis couldn't see *anything*.

He kept moving and moving until he tripped and rolled into the deep snow. He attempted to put his hand on the ground to get back on his feet, but his hand found nothing. He was on the edge of a cliff. Below him was nothing but the vast wilderness of the Icelandic terrain. Then, he turned around and saw a group of people holding knives, pitchforks, and torches. They were staring at him, not saying a single word.

Calvin emerged from the crowd, his two Angels following him. He looked at Lewis, shook his head in disappointment, and let out a weird grunt. His two Angels stepped forward and grabbed the professor. He tried to fight back. He screamed and kicked, but nothing worked.

He was being dragged back to Blackgate, and he had no idea what sort of hell was waiting for him there.

*

Karissa and Bolton exited the plane, the pilots watching them every step of the way. It was a cool, crisp morning, and the seagulls were cawing. They walked toward the small town of Dalvik, ready for anything.

Bolton turned around and saw the agents who had accompanied them staring hauntingly from the plane. Karissa noticed as well. She looked at Bolton and asked, "So they aren't coming with us?"

"No." Bolton paused. "We're on our own."

They both figured that the agents were part of the cult, considering the fact that, for starters, the FBI had been so quick to help them get to Iceland in the first place. And when neither of the two agents nor the pilots said anything to them the entire flight, it pretty much confirmed it.

Karissa and Bolton, they were meant to be here, and they knew it.

They kept walking until they reached town, where they saw a small red building and headed in that direction.

"Do you think anybody here even knows where this place is?" Karissa mumbled to Bolton, attempting to stay quiet.

"At this point, I don't care if they can hear us," Bolton said. "We are going to come face-to-face with them either way. We just need to make sure it's on our terms, considering we have no idea what's waiting for us."

They entered the small red building and saw a tiny old man behind the counter. He said something in Icelandic, most likely a greeting. Bolton looked around and asked, in English, if he knew where Blackgate was. The man had no idea what Bolton was saying until he heard the word "Blackgate." Then his eyes lit up, and he began to say a bunch of words in Icelandic. The man was now acting hysterical—he got up and shoved Karissa and Bolton out of his shop. He locked the door behind them.

Karissa looked at Bolton. "Well, I guess we're in the right place."

Bolton nodded in agreement. He looked around, attempting to find his next lead. Then, down the street, his eyes caught a person in a black robe. The stranger was staring at him from afar, not even attempting to hide. Bolton felt a small itch at the base of his skull.

"Karissa," he said softly.

She looked over and noticed the person.

"You ready?" Bolton asked her, still making eye contact with the robed figure.

"Why the hell not?" Karissa replied, taking a deep breath.

They started down the street toward the person. When they got about halfway there, the person turned and walked behind a building.

Karissa started to yell, but Bolton stopped her with his hand. He then gripped the pistol that rested on his hip. They kept walking cautiously, but then, out of nowhere, a black truck peeled out from behind the building up the road, throwing snow and dirt up into the air.

They began to run after it, and once they arrived at the spot where the truck had pulled out, both Bolton and

Karissa stopped in their tracks. As they breathed in the cold, Icelandic air, Karissa looked behind the building and noticed another black truck.

It was already running.

They knew what it meant. They got in, buckled up, and sped down the same road. As Karissa looked in the review mirror, she could see a crowd of people behind them, staring as they drove away.

# ~ 9 ~

Bolton pressed his foot hard onto the gas pedal, trying to keep up with the truck in front of them. He looked at Karissa.

"Hey," he started, "you need to be ready for anything, you understand?"

She looked at him. Beads of sweat were racing down the side of his face despite the freezing air.

"I'm ready," she responded.

Bolton was unconvinced, but he put his eyes back on the road. "Karissa. I mean, you need to be ready for *anything.*" He put emphasis on the final word.

She understood that they were running straight into a trap. She understood that she might be heading to her death. She understood that there was a possibility her husband, her Lewy, was already dead.

She noticed something about herself though. She'd spent this entire time afraid. Worried. Uncertain. But now, the thought of everything just pissed her off. She felt strong. Alive. Free.

Karissa Nelson was going to stand up and fight for her husband.

*Keep going north*, she thought to herself.

She looked in the back seat and saw the guns sitting in the duffel bag they had brought.

"I'm ready," she said coldly.

Her voice sent chills down Bolton's spine. But were the chills he felt from Karissa's words? Or something else?

*

When Lewis was brought back to Blackgate the night before, he was thrown into a cell. It was fairly small and had a bucket in the corner, as well as a bale of hay. He was frozen to the bone, but a few of the village women had brought in large pails of hot steaming water. They gave him a disgusting look before they left.

Lewis looked up to see Calvin entering the cell, waiving his hand to the same two Angels who always followed him around. They stopped immediately outside of the small room.

Lewis was shaking on the floor. "Leave me ALONE!" he screamed.

Calvin sat on the hay bale and let out a sigh. "You see," he began, "I simply cannot do that. Artemis' wish—"

"Fuck Artemis!" Lewis screamed. He attempted to stand up, but it was immediately followed by a backhand slap from Calvin, knocking Lewis to the floor.

"Listen to me, you ignorant, small child! You are nothing! Artemis is EVERYTHING! If you were not so important to him, I would peel every inch of your pathetic flesh from your bones and feed the rest of you to the SWINE!" Calvin screamed.

Then he cleared his throat.

"I'm sorry," he continued, "I believe it is time to share who our king truly is. I will explain further."

Lewis, frozen in fear, had blood streaming from his nose. He had no choice but to listen to Calvin.

"Our king was brought into this world in a village not far from where we are now. It was a village of liars and cheaters. They would steal each other's belongings; they would rape each other's wives. As a boy our king had a cleft lip and a nub for a hand. This was partially due to his parents being siblings. In fact, the whole village was family, but if a child was deformed, they would be executed, as they offered no use to the village. However, the young king's father, Uther, spared the boy. He told his son that he was going to be a king one day despite his deformities. Still, the king grew up tormented and teased. Everyone said he could not become a warrior, considering his deformities."

Calvin cleared his throat, then continued.

"A few years passed, and the boy was a man. He was in line to be the next king of the village, and he vowed to bring justice and prosperity to all the townspeople. Some of his 'family' didn't agree; they thought him weak, so they betrayed him. They burned the boy's house down, killing both of his parents. He survived, however, and the rest of the family took it upon themselves to throw the—as they called him—'demon born' off a cliff, the very cliff you almost fell off of tonight. When he hit the bottom, he was dying. Slowly, painfully, alone. Then, out of nowhere, a god dressed in gold appeared and said that the boy could live as long as he did one thing."

Calvin paused, almost as if he were waiting for Lewis to answer. But he didn't, so the man continued.

"Give up his soul. So, the boy did, and he vowed to avenge his parents. It is a night we remember here as Uthersday. The day the boy became our true King Artemis, the day he began his conquest to clear the world of those who are unworthy. The boy grew a hand, and his cleft lip disappeared, leaving only but a scar. So began Artemis' great conquest to cleanse this world—his world—of those who do not belong."

Calvin licked his lips then continued.

"During the midst of his conquest, however, Artemis felt weak; he was growing older. His alchemists were able to find a way to keep him alive forever. The secret to immortality no matter what happens. They gave him a drink made from flowers and obsidian they gathered from the volcano Grimsvotn. It stopped his heart, and he died. However, his soul still belonged to the God he gave it to, so after a few moments he returned to this world. He felt stronger. More powerful, as though his body had been molded from the obsidian and ash of the volcano. He then decided that he was going to conquer England. He used runes and dark magic, and he was unstoppable—until his power became too strong for some, and his own men decided to turn on him. His own followers killed Artemis' body and burned it while he was asleep."

"My god," Lewis finally said. But Calvin continued.

"Fortunately, he had many followers who believed in his way. They were able to use the dark magic and runes to make contact with Artemis' soul. It sat in the lands between the living and the dead where he remains to this day. He told his followers what to do next: cleanse the world of any and all those who do not belong here. Those that share the same qualities of the people that betrayed him. We lived in the shadows until the moment was right. Artemis needs a body to return to. A strong body, as well as a strong mind, but it must also be weak enough that he can take full control. This is your destiny, Lewis. You are feeling him guide you. You are the chosen one. Our Angels are guided by only him, and they chose not to cleanse your soul that night. You are meant for Artemis. He is to take over your soul and body so that he may live again on this earth and officially rule as he was once supposed to."

Lewis froze. This was it. He didn't want to believe this story, considering how far-fetched it seemed, but everything that was said to happen was happening, wasn't it? The fact that he wasn't in control of himself sometimes. The fact that he saw the vision of a Viking king. The fact that he was here when he didn't want to be. The fact that he left his lovely wife. It was true.

"What about my wife? And Bolton?" Lewis asked, his eyes glued to the floor.

"You will see them tomorrow, actually," Calvin said with a smile.

"Wait, what?" Lewis looked up with fire in his eyes.

"I told you they were coming, dear boy. And I do believe they are on a plane right now and will be here by morning." Calvin stood up.

Lewis shot up after him, but he was instantly backhanded to the face again. Calvin then left the cell. They locked the door and left Lewis to scream and shout himself into exhaustion.

\*

Karissa and Bolton looked at the entrance to Blackgate with wide eyes. They were stopped at the front gate as they watched the truck they were following drive through to the inside of the village. Before they even attempted to make their next move, a tall bald man in a black robe walked between them and the gates. Karissa's eyes were glued to the man as she asked Bolton what to do.

He replied, "Be cool. Whatever they do, follow along with it."

Sure enough, the man looked off to his side, and two Angels walked out from behind the sides of the gate toward the truck. Karissa's hands began to shake, as the Angels were horrifying to look at, even with their tall black pointy hoods on.

The Angels opened the truck doors from both sides and waited for Karissa and Bolton to get out. Bolton realized the bag of guns would be lost. His only weapon was the handgun he had on him. As they got out of the truck, the Angels immediately put black sacks over their heads, not allowing anybody to look at them.

Neither Karissa nor Bolton made a sound as the Angels patted them down. Their large boney hands felt everywhere on the two companions until the one with Bolton found his gun. He let out a quick groan. Bolton was listening intently to see if he could hear the sound of the gun being thrown, but he heard nothing. He thought to himself, *He must've kept it. Good.*

The Angels began to guide them through the gates. They could not see or hear anything besides the sound of their feet crunching the snow. The ominous silence was devastating. Especially to Karissa, who was trying her hardest to keep it together. She was on the verge of snapping. Not out of fear, but anger. She wanted to burn the whole place down and walk out of there in Lewis' arms.

The walk seemed very long. Both of the captives were lost in their own thoughts. Bolton was thinking about his wife and kids. He had a family to look after. He realized how stupid this was, how much of an idiot he was for doing this to his family.

*Why the hell am I here? Is this the right move? The right thing to do?* he thought to himself.

Then he thought about how this cult had roots in everything. Without his and Lewis' findings, the cult would've kept moving forward. Kept killing. Kept *cleansing.* And Bolton didn't know who he could trust. He felt it was his responsibility.

Suddenly, Karissa and Bolton were stopped and pushed to their knees. The sacks were quickly pulled from their heads, and they both adjusted their eyes to the bright shine of the snow that had fallen the night before.

Once their eyes focused, they noticed in front of them a bald man with a red robe that featured a black spiral on his chest. Behind him were two very tall men, obviously Angels, with their black pointed hoods over their grotesque faces.

"Hello," the bald man said with a very large smile. "You must be Andrew." After examining Bolton for a while, he looked over to Karissa. "And you must be Karissa Nelson."

He got extremely close to both of them, then he continued.

"It is very nice to meet the both of you. I am Calvin. I am the father of this here organization. You must have plenty of questions! Who we are, why we're here, what our purpose—"

Karissa cut him off. "Where is my husband?" she said coldly, staring straight into Calvin's soul.

"Ah, yes," Calvin said, tilting his head slightly toward her. Before he answered, he lowered himself into a squat so he was eye level with Karissa. He was so close to her face, she could taste his breath. "Lewis has been awfully naughty since his arrival. You'd have been proud of him. Alas, we are not. In fact, we are extremely angry with him, but when everything begins to come to fruition like it is, there are bound to be complications."

Calvin shot up and looked at the crowd of people behind them. Karissa and Bolton had no idea they were there because they had been so quiet.

"Today is the day, my children! Today we celebrate the changing of this world! Back to the old king. Back to Artemis! We shall prepare! The Cleansing is nigh!"

The crowd made a simultaneous gasping sound, followed by a thump to their chest. Calvin turned around and walked through the doors of the black church. He waved his hand, and the Angels picked Karissa and Bolton up and dragged them into the church behind him.

Inside, there were thousands of lit red candles. Red banners with black spirals filled the room. Calvin stood there, intimidating.

"First up, the detective," he said softly.

# ~ 10 ~

Agents Phil and Bobby had just come from telling the FBI director their findings. He looked over the book and created a plan to take down every single person whose name was listed. This included senators, governors, mayors, police chiefs, firefighters, doctors, journalists, and even scientists. A black ops task force would be created to take care of each and every one of them as soon as possible.

They knew the cult could strike at any moment, so there was no time for discussions or debates. The people whose names were written in the book needed to be removed from their positions of power as quickly as possible.

They wanted to wipe this cult from the face of the earth and bring the world out of darkness. Therefore, they named the task force "White Light." Agent Phil and Agent Bobby were leading.

They did not need to play by the rules, as the Angels of Artemis had now been classified as a terrorist organization. They knew it was going to take a long time, but the fact that they had the green light to take down any one of these cult members put a smile on Agent Phil's face.

Phil and a few other agents were walking in a hallway of the Portland Police Department, suited up in SWAT gear.

"Although I still think you need to take a few days to recover, I applaud your initiative, Phil. We are really doing this," Bobby said.

"Yeah, if only Bolton were here. He'd be proud. I hope they are doing okay."

"I'm sure Bolton is fine. I'm sure the Nelsons are fine. Let's just go do our job and dissolve the cult."

Phil smiled and said, "All right. Let's go."

*

It was a cold morning in Portland. The rain had turned to snow, although none of it was sticking to the ground. The agents were on the move. Their first stop was a small office building near downtown. Agent Phil was in the back of an armored van with five other men, all highly geared up. Some were loaded up with M4 assault rifles and others with MP5 submachine guns.

Agent Bobby was leading his team of five armed men around behind the office building. The person inside was a journalist for the local newspaper. His name was John Finch, and according to the journal in Byrd's house, he'd been a member of the Angels of Artemis for seven years.

Phil's team got the green light and broke through the office doors. There wasn't anybody there, and the lights were off. Phil and his men kept their guns up and ready to fire. He held up his fist to tell his men to hold. He heard a loud bang from the floor above him. They kept moving through the building, but it was terribly quiet. Not a single soul in sight.

Phil got up to the second floor and noticed a slight cry coming from a room. He and his men slowly walked through. They made sure to check all corners to cut down on the chance of any surprises. The room featured cubicles and a copier machine. He checked a few of the desks and was surprised to see one with a nameplate that spelled out "K. Nelson."

Phil continued until he was close to the sound of the cry. When he turned the corner, he noticed a man with duct tape around his mouth. His eyes grew wide when he saw Phil, and he shook his head when the FBI agent approached him. Phil ripped the tape off, and the man said, "Behind you."

Suddenly, another man came out from the corner of the room with a knife. As he swung it, the knife glided through Phil's sleeve. The man's attack was quickly thwarted when three bullets entered his chest from one of Phil's men. The man lay there in a rapidly growing pool of blood. Phil used the opportunity to quickly ask the dying man a question.

"Where did Commissioner Byrd run off to?"

The man smiled while a stream of blood leaked from the corner of his mouth. "It's too...late...for you all. Cleanse... cle..." His body went limp as he died.

Agent Bobby and his men entered the room. He took off his helmet and goggles and looked at the dead cult member before him.

"Well, one down, a lot more to go." He put his helmet back on and waved his hand in a circle, telling his men to re-group back at their base. He was about to cut the duct-taped man free, but Phil, still looking at the body, said, "Wait. It's too easy."

Bobby looked at Phil with confusion. "What do you mean?"

Phil looked over at the captive man and said, "The man over there, I think he knew we were coming."

Bobby looked at the man as well. "You think he's in on it?"

The man looked up at the two armed agents and said in a shaky voice, "No, please. I have no idea what happened. I barely knew that man! He worked in the building, but I had no idea."

Phil knew they couldn't take any chances. He told the man to calm down, but that he needed to come in for further questions.

*

Later, back at White Light's base of operations, Phil and Bobby were sitting at a table in a white room. Across from them was the man who'd been captured by John Finch. His name was George. Phil made sure that George was calm and ready to answer any questions, and he did just that. He explained that John had been called into their managing director's office. After some time, John went back to his seat, and the managing director told everyone they could have the rest of the day off.

George had been gathering his things when he was knocked out, and he awoke in a dark building, wrapped up in duct tape. George also said that John had been talking quietly to himself, saying that the piggies were on their way, that the Cleansing was here, and that was time to cleanse.

Phil and Bobby asked George if they could have the managing director's name.

George told them his name was Jack Garcia.

*

Phil was in his car, a black SUV, eating a burrito and going over his notes. He realized that Jack Garcia was also the name of Lewis' boss, however, the name was not on the list. If Jack was a part of the cult, there were more members out there who were not listed.

Phil received a call from Agent Bobby, who told him that apparently, after Jack's wife's parents were found dead, Lisa had a mental breakdown, and Jack couldn't handle it. There were multiple calls from Lisa Garcia to the Portland Police Department about her husband going crazy.

Apparently, Jack left and never said a thing to anybody. Lisa didn't file a missing person's report, but his absence from his job at the university was on file.

Agent Phil told Bobby he was heading to the Garcias' house, and Bobby was going to the university to ask around.

Phil was growing tired. After everything he had been through, he was hoping, praying, that Jack could somehow lead to the downfall of the cult. He got in his car and began to think about Bolton and the Nelsons. Hoping to god they were okay. Little did he know what was in store for him.

*

Karissa had just been punched in the face by an Angel. Bolton screamed out the various ways he'd make them pay for that until he, too, was struck in the jaw and knocked to the floor of the church. Blood dripped from his mouth. He let out a groan of pain but looked up at the Angel who hit him. The tall, mutilated being still held Bolton's handgun in the belt of his black robe.

Bolton looked at Calvin, who was beginning to say some words at the altar. Bolton couldn't understand since they were in a different language, but he knew they couldn't be good.

Karissa looked around. She began to realize their situation. Angels surrounded them in the church. The people who flooded the rest of the church and out to the street began to hum and chant. Calvin began to sing in an ominous tone. Karissa knew something horrible was about to happen.

Calvin then stopped his singing, turned around, and said, "Bring in our Savior!"

Two more Angels walked in from the back of the church. They held Lewis, who was absolutely battered and bruised. His feet were blue and purple from the night before, when he'd been running through the snow barefoot. His white robe was now filthy, covered in dirt and blood. He saw his wife. Right there in front of him, on her knees, bleeding from a cut above her eye.

Karissa let out a gasp and called out for him, but she was quickly struck again. Lewis, even with his black eye and frostbitten feet, screamed and attempted to fight back after seeing what had just happened to his wife.

"I'll fucking kill you!" he screamed until one of the Angels punched him in the back of the head, stunning him.

"We are gathered her today," Calvin began, "to bear witness to our purpose. TODAY, WE WITNESS THE RETURN OF OUR GREAT SAVIOR AND HUMBLE KING, ARTEMIS!"

Lewis shook his head and looked at Bolton and Karissa. Tears streamed from his face as he saw his beautiful wife and his new friend, both on the ground in beaten states. All because of him. The guilt couldn't match anything he had ever felt before.

"I'm so sorry," he said to them both.

Calvin pulled out the Herja and began to read.

Karissa looked at her husband. Love filled her gaze like it was her first time seeing him. But a stone-cold sadness filled her heart as she realized this could be the last time she would ever see him.

Calvin continued to read from the Herja, and the villagers throughout Blackgate chanted and hummed.

"I love you, Lewis Nelson," Karissa said to her husband.

But Lewis' eyes had rolled to the back of his head. The itch at the base of his skull was now covering his entire body. It was too overbearing. Lewis was being pushed farther and farther away from reality.

His body began to contort and bend in ways the human body shouldn't. He groaned and drooled and rolled around.

"Lewis. Baby, what's wrong?" Karissa said with tears streaming down her face. "Stop this, please," she said, looking at Calvin.

Lewis began to seize and shake until...

It wasn't Lewis anymore.

Bolton knew it was over. He couldn't save his friend anymore. But he could do what Lewis would've wanted. He could burn Blackgate to the ground and get Karissa to safety.

Lewis let out an otherworldly roar, which quieted everyone in the village, including Calvin. After a few more moments of chanting and singing and Lewis' body shaking and twisting, everyone stopped instantly.

"My children...I am home," A voice said coming out of Lewis' body except it wasn't his own. This voice was deep and raspy.

Calvin bowed down, and the rest of the crowd did the same. Calvin began to speak. "My lord, your form needs to be cleansed. The woman is the only thing he's ever loved. Cleanse her, and Lewis will be forgotten, as you will sever his mind from the body, and you will be in full control. The Cleansing is set to begin shortly to finish the ritual."

Artemis put a hand on his head in pain. "This body and mind are strong. The Cleansing must begin now. What of the other?" He gestured to Bolton.

"He is to be your new Angel. His haunted past makes his mind perfect for the procedure. He will become the best Angel we have ever created."

The Angels picked up Karissa first and dragged her closer to Artemis. Bolton screamed out in anger as two other Angels grabbed him and began to drag him behind the altar to the back of the church His scream faded as he was dragged into a different room.

Artemis grabbed a knife from the altar. The blade was painted red. Karissa began to call out to Lewis.

"Honey, I know you're in there!" she screamed. "I need you to fight, Lewis! Fight!"

"Hush now, child," Artemis said, smiling. "He is..."

The smile faded as he stumbled and put his hand on his head again. He collected himself and stood tall. He attempted to raise the knife, but he began twitching.

Confused and uncertain, Artemis needed more strength. He passed Karissa, walked out of the church doors, and stood tall above the village. Everyone's eyes were on him.

"Quiet now everyone," he said stumbling a bit more. "The ritual must be completed, the Cleansing shall begin. It is time, my children! Begin the Cleanse!"

Everyone cheered as Artemis returned to the altar, where he stood beside Calvin.

Calvin walked to the side of the church, where a large black and red horn wound its way up to the ceiling. He took a deep breath and exhaled for as long as he could into the horn.

Karissa screamed Lewis' name as Artemis stepped close to her and held the knife to her throat. Bolton was led down a flight of stairs and into a large white room that looked like a laboratory. He then saw the table he would be tied down to. He looked at one of the Angels that was holding him and noticed his pistol still tucked in its belt.

After a long moment, the sound of the horn stopped.

The Cleansing had begun.

*

Agent Phil was almost to the Garcias' house. The sun was setting, and a wall of clouds turned everything a dark shade of orange. Phil had an uneasy feeling. As he drove up the driveway, he noticed how nice and big the Garcias' house was. He got out of his car and walked to the front door.

It was cracked open.

*What the hell?*

He put his hand on his sidearm and walked to the door. He knocked, but there was no answer.

"Hello?" Phil said loudly. "Mr. and Mrs. Garcia?"

After pure silence, Phil heard a very loud scream from somewhere in the neighborhood that made him jump. He surveyed the area around him, then turned his attention back to the Garcias' home.

He decided to enter, and he was in pure shock at the scene that lay before him.

The only light came from a lamp that was facing a wall where a large red spiral had been painted with blood.

And Lisa Garcia was hanging right beside it.

Phil sighed and realized that this confirmed that Jack Garcia was part of the cult. It proved that there were countless individuals involved, and not just the ones whose names were written in the journal.

*BOOM!!!*

Phil jumped at the sound of an explosion. He sprinted out of the house to see what it was. Explosions were going off near downtown Portland, followed by the sounds of gunshots and sirens.

Phil exited the house and watched the Portland skyline. In a matter of seconds, the city became a complete warzone. He realized that if the cult had an endgame, this would be it. Every member had awoken and taken up arms. They were killing people in the streets, blowing up buildings.

Phil felt a wave of hopelessness crash over him. The end of the world had begun.

# ~ 11 ~

The city was on fire.

The world was on fire. Cities, farms, neighborhoods, all victims to a raging inferno.

Nancy Collins, a forty-one-year-old schoolteacher was in the process of stabbing her husband, screaming the word "cleanse." Jason Parker, a twenty-eight-year-old gas station employee, killed everyone in the store then drenched the whole place in gasoline. He pulled out his lighter and caused the gas station to blow up in a massive explosion. Tommy Moore, a fifty-six-year-old veteran, was standing in the street in a red pointed hood and robes. He was commanding about ten people in black hooded robes to open fire on the city.

Agent Phil drove his black SUV straight into the thick of it. He called on his radio for backup from White Light, but all he got was static. He checked his back seat to make sure he had his M4A1 and plenty of ammo.

*If I'm going out, I'm taking some of you bastards with me,* he thought.

As he drove onto the bridge that led downtown, all he saw were bodies and fire. He kept driving until he saw somebody worth either saving or killing. Sure enough, a few moments later, a young woman ran out into the middle of the street screaming for help. Two black-robed and hooded figures were following her.

Phil came to a screeching stop and grabbed his M4. He exited the car in a hurry and pointed the gun at the men.

"Hey! Over here!" he screamed.

The woman noticed him and began sprinting toward him. Phil began firing shots at the hooded people. Three shots hit and killed one of them. Two more shots, including one to the head, instantly dropped the other.

The woman kept running even though the threat had been eradicated. Phil spoke up and told the woman that she was okay.

She kept running.

"Let's get out of here, okay? I'll take you to safe—"

Before he could finish, she let out a scream and jumped on Phil. They both launched back into the side of his SUV. The M4 slid under the car. Phil let out a grunt but had no time to collect his thoughts as the woman jumped right back up and onto him. Then she pulled out a knife and began to cut Phil's forearms, which he'd held up in defense.

Phil realized what he had to do and that he needed to do it quickly. He grabbed her hand that held the knife and forced it away from him. She used her other hand to continuously scratch his face, until Phil grabbed his sidearm from his holster and put three shots into her stomach.

She groaned and fell over.

Phil got up immediately and looked at the woman he had just killed. She was screaming for help, but Phil understood now that she was bait, and the hooded figures following her were meant to cleanse whoever helped her.

Phil felt blood seeping through a large scratch on his cheek. He shook his head then picked up his M4 from under the SUV. He decided to ditch the car and continued down the street on foot. As he walked, more bodies began to pile up on the streets. The pops of gunshots rang in his ears. It sounded like a full-on war was in progress.

Phil ran toward the sound to see if he could help. He happened upon an intersection in which, sure enough, a firefight was taking place. Three white police cars were parked near each other with about six officers hiding behind them. On the opposing side, about fifteen black hooded figures were shooting back. They had no cover and did not need it, as the continuous firing at the officers did not allow for any return fire. Phil could see a few dead officers who'd tried to interrupt the bombardment of bullets but failed. The cultists were inching closer and closer, firing their weapons and reloading continuously.

Phil quickly aimed his M4 at them, but something held him back. The woman he had just saved tried to kill him. He knew that if it was a trap, there would be fifteen cult members as well as six pretend officers on his ass. He waited a moment longer and then made a choice. He cocked his M4 and began to shoot at the cultists.

Two of them were killed instantly by headshots. Another was shot in the neck, and he fell to his knees and bled out right in front of the others. They all noticed this and turned to Phil, who was still shooting. Another's head was separated from her shoulders. They all began to shoot at Phil, who took notice and ran to the side of the road, where he hid behind a car.

The police officers noticed that the bullets had stopped coming for them and were now directed down another street. They used this opportunity to get up and begin their attack. Three cult members dropped pretty quickly as the officers began their own parade of bullets. Phil got up and returned fire as well, killing another two.

The cultists became flustered, as they were not sure which direction to shoot in. The officers dropped another two before an extremely loud engine could be heard from a distance.

The cultists immediately stopped shooting, lowered their guns, and kneeled. Phil stopped shooting, too, as did the other officers, although their guns were still locked on the cultists.

Phil got out from behind the car and began moving toward the officers, his gun still facing the cultists. The engine became louder and louder. Then they began to hear what sounded like a 1940s song over an intercom. It was faint, but it got louder as the engines did.

"Something's coming," Phil told the officers as he grouped up with them. "Reload and get ready."

Three large trucks turned down the street. Each had about six hooded figures in the back. The truck in the middle was larger than the rest, and a man in a red hood and robe was standing in the back.

Phil and the other officers hid behind the police cars for more cover. Their guns were now aimed at the trucks. The ones who were kneeling began to hum and chant words Phil could not understand.

One of the police officers said, "Steady, men."

The vehicles had all come to a stop and the cultists got out of the trucks. Each was holding an assault rifle or shotgun. The 1940s song continued to play over the intercom of the middle truck. Phil could not understand any of the words, as the song was in a different language.

The red-hooded individual got out of the back of his truck and walked closer. One of the black-hooded cultists walked up and kneeled before him. He presented the red-hooded man with a black AK-47 with a red spiral painted on it. The man grabbed the gun and cocked it.

"Agent Phil!" the red-hooded man said.

Phil, obviously caught off guard, took a moment to speak. "Yeah?" he finally yelled back.

"I only want to talk. Please show yourself."

"Not a chance in hell, prick!" Phil replied.

"Fine," the man said. "No more false faces!" He then proceeded to remove his hood. Phil looked through the broken window of the police cruiser to see none other than Commissioner Byrd.

The man who handed Byrd his rifle also unmasked himself. Phil was filled with rage—it was Jack Garcia.

Phil stood up. "Did you have fun killing your wife, you sick bastard?"

Jack shook his head, "She was weak, Agent Phil."

Byrd spoke loudly. "Everything we have done, everything we live for, it is all because of him, our king."

"Who, Artemis?" Phil began to laugh. "You guys realize that's a girl's name, right?"

Every single hooded figure let out a deep huff. Jack looked as though he'd bit his tongue, and Byrd spit at the ground.

"I will let that slide, Phil," Byrd began, "as you will be cleansed momentarily."

"I wouldn't count on it," Phil said angrily.

"You need to understand our glorious achievement," Jack started. "As the world is being cleansed, you no longer need to fight. Look around you. Everything you have worked for is being demolished. Your friends are being sacrificed as we speak."

"Wait, what do you mean?" Phil yelled.

"Well, Artemis has returned to this world in Lewis' physical form," Byrd said. "He needs only to kill Mr. Nelson's wife, then Karissa and he will be in this world forever. The Cleansing lets Artemis gain the necessary power to complete the ritual. Andrew Bolton will be dissected, and he'll have the pleasure of being Artemis' guardian Angel."

"Yeah, I don't think so!" Phil screamed while standing up and aiming at them. He began to fire, killing three cultists instantly. The officers began to fire as well. An all-out war began in the city of Portland. Bullets were hitting the police cars, sending pieces of metal into the air. Phil ducked down for a moment to reload his M4. An officer got shot in the head and fell down in front of him, blood pooling out. Phil looked upon the dead officer with wide eyes. The wave of cultists kept coming closer, as they knew there was nowhere for Phil and the officers to run.

Phil looked around him. Another officer had been shot in the neck, and he flew into the street with great force. Portland was burning. There was no way out. When Phil decided to get back up and shoot back, he realized that he and one other officer were the only ones left standing. He began to shoot while letting out a scream. The bullets of his M4 cut through the bodies and skulls of three cultists like it was nothing.

One of the bullets Phil fired hit Jack Garcia square in the face. Byrd took notice, as his comrade had fallen to the ground in a gurgling mess. Byrd lifted his rifle and aimed it at the agent.

Phil continued to fire until he was hit in his shoulder, sending him flying onto his back. The bullet had come from Byrd's AK. The other officer wasn't so lucky, as five bullets from multiple cultists had hit him in the chest, neck, and head, killing him.

Now Phil was the only one who remained.

The firing stopped at once. There were no sounds of celebration by the cultists, no explosions, nothing. Complete silence. Agent Phil looked around. His M4 was about eight feet from where he was lying. He tried to reach it, but the pain of the bullet lodged into his shoulder wouldn't allow him to.

He still had his sidearm, which he pulled out, getting ready for the army of cultists to inevitably come around the wall of battered police cruisers that separated them. Sure enough, a few moments later, that's exactly what happened.

They all had their guns aimed at him. Phil figured that even though he could probably only take down one or two more of the cultists before they started firing at him, they were probably going to kill him anyway, so he began to shoot.

Two of them dropped dead, but the others did not move at all. They had absolutely no fear of dying.

When Phil's handgun locked in the cocked-back position, signifying that he had run out of ammo, he just lay there and looked at the barrel, which was still smoking.

"Ah, screw it," he said as he threw it to his side and looked up into the sky.

Blood was pouring out of his shoulder, causing the pool that formed below him to spread. Byrd jumped on the cop car in front of him, his red robe flowing in the wind and ash.

"Well, Agent Phil, here we are," Byrd began as he kneeled down on the hood. "I could leave you here to die, or I could save you, and you could join us. Which would you prefer?" He looked deep into Phil's eyes.

"Enough with the theatrics. Just kill me, you pathetic bastard," Phil said, struggling to get the words out. "But just know one thing: you will lose. If you think that Andrew Bolton will go down without a fight then you are gravely mistaken. If you think this world will succumb to your laughable ideas... then you are about as stupid as they come."

"Hm," Byrd mumbled. "So be it."

After a brief moment, Jack aimed his AK-47 and shot seven bullets into Agent Phil, killing him instantly. And as Phil's body lay there in the middle of a burning Portland, Commissioner Byrd and the rest of his cultists hopped back into their trucks and drove off, looking to do some more cleansing.

*

Bolton lay on an ice-cold table. He was strapped in and couldn't move. The Angels had led him through a long set of stairs, down a hallway and under the chapel before entering a cold white room that was lit up like a laboratory. There, they threw him onto the table and strapped him in.

The two Angels stood at the door and did nothing more. Bolton looked over at the one who had his pistol in his belt.

It was still there.

The sound of a door opening startled Bolton. A small bald man walked through. He was wearing a black lab coat. Bolton noticed a large lump on the man's right shoulder, which wasn't covered. He showed disgust on his face as the man approached him.

"Hello, Detective Bolton," the man said in an Icelandic accent. "I am Gunther. I have been healing this village for many, many years, and let me just say: you have been given a huge gift. What an honor it is to be the personal Angel of Artemis."

"You're going to turn me into one of those freaks?" Bolton asked nervously, gesturing towards the two Angels.

Gunther slapped him hard, leaving a bright red mark on his face. "They are my perfections, you swine!"

"Y'all really like slapping, huh?" Bolton said, shaking his head.

Gunther opened a drawer that contained a plethora of tools. Once Bolton saw them, he nervously asked, "Okay, but why me?"

"Andrew Bolton, in order to make an Angel, we need a strong body that can survive the modifications. The mind needs to be strong as well, and severe trauma makes a mind strong. We've been watching you for a long, long time."

"What do you mean?" Bolton asked.

"The Curry family that you killed in Montana; they were members of ours."

Bolton's shocked look said it all. "What are you saying?"

Gunther put his tools down and walked over to Bolton. He sat down and looked into his eyes. "They followed Artemis' guidance, my friend. The problem was they were extremists."

Bolton laughed. "Wait, you're telling me you guys aren't extremists?"

Gunther continued, "They wished for the Cleansing to come early, thinking that performing the Cleansing would be the thing that brings Artemis back to us instead of waiting patiently for the right mind and body to come around. So, they would go around cleansing whomever they deemed worthy. When the daughter came to her senses and decided she wanted to wait until the actual Cleansing, she ran away and joined another family we had there. She sparked up a relationship with the boy of that family and stayed in their home. The rest of the Currys didn't like that, and, well, you know the rest. So when you killed them, we knew it would leave just the right amount of trauma to make you a perfect Angel. Especially with the death of your parents. However, you left, and we lost track of you until we recruited you. We figured that perfect balance of strength and damage would be very suitable for Artemis."

"Wait," Bolton started, "what do you mean you recruited me?"

"Andrew," Gunther said softly. "We were the ones who helped you become an FBI agent."

Bolton sat there in disbelief. He felt as though his whole life was a lie. He couldn't speak for a long moment until he noticed Gunther fidgeting with his tools again.

"Okay, so if it's trauma that makes us good a fit, why is Lewis the one Artemis chose?"

"Why?" Gunther asked as Bolton continued to nervously watch him examine his materials. "There are things in Lewis' past that we were not aware of. Things that quickly presented themselves to us after that night when Mr. Hopkins was cleansed. Just like you, Andrew, he is haunted by a dark past."

Gunther put down his tools and sat next to the operating table. He looked the detective deep in his eyes.

"Back when Lewis was a child, he and his brother were walking home from school, and a few bullies jumped them. Well, the brother told Lewis to fight, but, alas, the young professor decided to run, leaving his brother outnumbered, if you will. The bullies ended up beating the brother to death. When they found little Lewis, they didn't beat him. No, they dragged him over to the brother's body and told him that if he told anybody, they would do the same to his family and friends and then finally Lewis himself. Lewis didn't know what to do, so he began to plot. As you are now aware, trauma is something we look for. However, Lewis' was different."

Gunther looked around in bliss, like he had just walked through a field of roses.

"Lewis' trauma built up inside of him. He didn't take it out on anyone. Not for a very long time. Add in a friend dead to suicide and dead parents to a car accident—not to mention the will to not act on your trauma—and you get something better: rage. The thing he has not told a single soul is that in college, he went back home, and while he was out at a bar by himself, the bullies that killed his brother walked in. The second Lewis saw them, he told them to meet him outside. Sure enough, the men did, and Lewis proceeded to use a broken bottle and his bare hands to kill two out of the three. He let the last one live and stated that if he told anybody, he would kill his friends, family, and then him."

"Jesus Christ," Bolton said out loud.

"But something changed Lewis," Gunther continued, "gave him a new take on life. It was his wife, Karissa. When they met in college, Lewis' rage took a back seat to his love for her. Sure, it would show itself sometimes, but only if there was a threat to Karissa. She was the one who kept him in line. We needed her gone in order for the trauma to set back in and the rage to take over. So, the plan was to dispatch Karissa, and as soon as Lewis found out, we'd sedate him and bring him here for Artemis. This, however, didn't work. Karissa left Spokane too early, and you and Lewis decided to run your own little investigation. Either way, Lewis is here, as are you and Karissa. Once Artemis kills her, Lewis will no longer be present. Artemis will have full control of his body, and we can finish the cleansing for a better world. For Artemis' world, as is his will."

"Well, that just sounds like the most bullshit thing I have ever heard," Bolton exclaimed.

Gunther gave a slight laugh and began to grab his tools. Bolton decided to start squirming on the table, making it hard for Gunther to begin his procedure. The Angels walked over to the table and held Bolton down.

The thing was, Bolton's hand was right next to his handgun, which still sat in the angel's belt. Bolton knew he had one chance. He wasn't sure how he was going to fight off two Angels and a doctor while he was strapped down, but he believed it would be better for him to die than be turned into an Angel.

He thought of his beautiful family. His two daughters and loving wife.

Then, Bolton quickly grabbed the gun, and, although restrained, he pointed it up into the Angel's abdomen and fired three times. The Angel fell back but didn't die. The other Angel must've been startled, as he grabbed the entire operating table, with Bolton on it, and threw it across the lab.

Gunther yelled at the Angel, "No! You stupid fool! You will destroy my work!"

Bolton lay there for a moment. The table was broken, and the straps were off. He was dazed but quickly snapped out of it. He saw the Angels and Gunther in front of him. When Gunther gave the order to seize the detective, Bolton grabbed the handgun and fired it into the first Angel's head, causing half of it to be blown off. He aimed at the second Angel and fired again, right through the head, killing him instantly.

Gunther put his hands up and after a short time, began laughing. "Quite poetic, isn't it?" he said, shaking.

Bolton aimed the gun at him and asked where Lewis and Karissa were. There was bloodlust in his eyes.

Gunther knew what was going to happen but continued anyway. "You will arrive to their rescue too late. And you believe the bullets you have left in that gun will be enough to kill us all? Think again, boy."

"You're right, guess I should save them," Bolton said fiercely.

He put the gun in his belt, then grabbed Gunther by the collar of his lab coat and looked at him in the eyes.

"I am also filled with rage..." the detective said before throwing the man against the wall, then quickly began to bash his head into it, over and over again, until half of Gunther's face was stained on the white wall.

Then Bolton began his way up to the main part of the chapel. Now that he knew the Cleansing was in full force, he knew his only hope at saving Lewis—and perhaps the whole world—was that Artemis had not killed Karissa yet.

*

She looked into his eyes. The eyes that were no longer his. While he still looked like Lewis, he spoke differently, and he acted with strange mannerisms that Lewis would never use. She was so drawn to the fact that her beloved was no longer hers that she'd completely ignored the words he was preaching to the village and the large knife he held in his hand.

She didn't care. She watched Artemis put both of his arms up as he soaked in the horrific chants of the villagers. Karissa wished for only one thing: that Lewis would be there too, wherever they might end up.

She was reminded of a time when she and Lewis were still young. It was their fourth date, and Lewis took her along the Oregon shoreline to a large, rustic bridge that sat right on the beach. The sun was setting, and the stars began to show themselves above. Karissa remembered lying down and looking at the gleaming lights above while holding Lewis' hand.

He was warm. She would always remember that warmth. The same warmth she would always feel when she was with him. She thought about the words he said to her that night. How some believe stars are souls. Shooting stars are souls who know exactly where they're going, and the ones we see every night are stuck between this world and the next because they are waiting for their soulmate to join them.

Karissa found this memory comforting. If Lewis' soul was still stuck in that body while Artemis used it, she would wait for him. That is what went through her head even when Artemis grabbed her by the neck and put the knife there. Her eyes were closed, as she didn't want to see what became of Lewis, she wanted to live their life together over and over again in her mind.

Before Artemis was able to slide the knife across her throat, a tear ran down her face all the way to his hand. Karissa whispered, "I love you..."

Artemis' eyes widened.

Once Lewis heard that and felt her tear touch his hand from the abyss where he was, he no longer felt as though he were in the trunk. Now, he felt like he was in the passenger seat. He looked Artemis right in his glowing red eyes...

"Hey there buddy," Lewis said with confidence. "Give me my fucking body back."

He punched Artemis, which caused the fight for Lewis' body to ensue. Karissa opened her eyes to the sound of Artemis grunting. He stepped away from her and began to grab his head. He was screaming.

Calvin nervously asked, "My Lord! Is everything all right?!"

Artemis ran into the altar, knocking it over, along with some candles. And before anyone knew it, rugs and curtains began to catch on fire. Karissa looked at everything with wide eyes. She wanted to help in any way she could.

So, she started speaking the truth.

"Lewy!" she screamed while watching Artemis fall down again, holding his head in agony. "You are my soulmate! The absolute love of my life! You need to come back to me! Come back to me, Lewy! I love you!"

Artemis' scream sounded like he was being dragged to hell. Inside his mind, Lewis was fighting back.

"You had your chance in this world," Lewis started as he grabbed Artemis by the horn and swung his face into his knee, "you blew it. You will not take me from her. I will fight for her until the end of time."

"This is impossible," Artemis said on his knees to Lewis. "I am a king!"

"No. You are a worthless and pathetic excuse for one," Lewis said, standing over Artemis' body.

"The world you live in needs me; it needs to be cleansed. These people lie and cheat. They care about none but themselves. Under my rule, they would be eradicated from existence."

"That's where you're wrong," Lewis said, stepping to Artemis. "Is the world full of assholes? You bet. But they don't deserve to die because of it. And you think people would change under your rule? No. We are human beings. Some are like that by nature but we all deserve the right to grow and learn from our mistakes."

"You fool," Artemis said with wide eyes.

"And on top of that, you hurt my wife, you piece of shit." Lewis grabbed Artemis by the head and snapped his neck, causing Artemis to flee Lewis' body.

*

During the fight for Lewis' body, two Angels grabbed Karissa off her knees and began to take her to the back of the chapel, which was now on fire.

"Get off of me!" she screamed at them.

She looked over at Lewis and saw him get up off the floor. He searched around until he saw her. They made eye contact. She knew his eyes. They were his eyes.

Lewis shot up and began to run after her until he was hit in the face with a log. He fell down hard but looked up to see the log being swung at him again. He rolled away just before the log crushed his face into the floor. He looked up to see none other than Calvin, holding a log from the burning church. Lewis got up again, blood streaming out of his nose.

"I'm not impressed," Calvin said. "You cannot stop Artemis, for he is all powerful."

"I stopped him already. He is not coming back, Calvin," Lewis responded. "If even he couldn't stop me from getting to Karissa, you definitely don't have a chance."

Calvin's response was to angrily swing the log again, but he missed, and Lewis dodged the attack. The professor punched the back of Calvin's head, causing him to stumble. Lewis began to run to the back of the church, until an Angel burst through the door, throwing Lewis halfway across the room. He looked up to see Calvin standing by an Angel while a tapestry with a red spiral on it burned up behind them.

Lewis looked around for any sort of weapon. Then he saw it. Right behind Calvin and the angel was the knife that he'd held when his body wasn't his. He shot straight forward and ran as fast as he could. Calvin lined up for a swing, but Lewis saw it coming and at the very last minute slid underneath both Calvin's swing and the Angel's large hand.

He grabbed the dagger and quickly swung around to stab the Angel's knee. The Angel fell like a rag doll, and Lewis pulled the knife out and quickly stabbed it in the face. It died immediately.

He knew Calvin was somewhere near him, but he couldn't pull the dagger out from the Angel's face fast enough, and he was hit in the side of his head.

"No!" Calvin screamed. "You horrendous little pig! That dagger is sacred!"

Lewis looked up dazed as Calvin hit him again. Blood from his mouth splattered the floor with another hit. And another. Lewis could hardly see out of his right eye. As Calvin raised the log for one final blow, a flaming piece of wood from the roof fell down and smashed in between the two, causing Calvin to fall down.

The entire chapel was coming down now. Lewis got up slowly and stepped over the wood to free the knife from the dead Angel's face. Calvin was attempting to get up until a kick to the head stopped him immediately. He turned around and saw a bleeding Lewis holding the sacred knife. He made one final statement.

"Whatever you do, Lewis, just know that you will not win. Artemis will come back. I swear it."

Lewis did not care. He grabbed Calvin by the top of his head and slit his throat as he stared into his eyes. Blood poured out as Calvin grabbed his severed throat. He fell over slowly and lay there until he died.

Lewis turned around and started for the back of the chapel, but he was quickly stopped short by a large burning log that had fallen in front of the door. The smell of burnt wood filled the air. Sparks were flying high. Smoke was fuming toward the hole in the roof and out into the world. Lewis ran back toward the front door, but he quickly realized that it was also blocked off.

He was stuck inside the burning chapel.

Looking around for another path, the professor went back toward the back door. And, while it was obviously still blocked off, there was a door that wasn't. Lewis opened it and saw a flight of stairs that was accompanied by a dark hallway. He looked back one more time to make sure it was his only option. Sure enough, it was. So Lewis started down the stairs and into the darkness.

*

Karissa was attempting to free herself from the Angels' grasp. They held on to her arms so tightly, she thought they might break them. Even through the sleeves of her shirt she could feel the long fingernails and the almost-rusty hands of the Angels.

They were taking her somewhere past the village. She was confused because the path led up a hill. She turned her head to look behind her, but all she could see was the massive snowstorm that was about to engulf the village and the chapel up in flames. And before she knew it, the chapel faded out with the fog of snow, and all that could be seen was the orange glow of the fire.

When they reached the top of the hill, Karissa realized that there was no more land to be walked. It was a cliff. She began to scream and attempted to wiggle out of the Angels' grasp, but their hands were locked on.

Tired of her struggling, they forced her to her knees, and she stopped fighting back. She realized they were not going to push her over the edge. It was something more. Perhaps a backup plan? The Angels then spun her around so she faced the chapel, which was now completely invisible. In fact, she had a hard time seeing five feet in front of her.

There was nothing but silence. The snowflakes were very large, and they stuck to the ground. There was a strong, ice-cold wind that made Karissa's brown hair dance. The Angels made no movements, no sounds, nothing. All she had to do was wait. For what was the question pouring fright into her mind.

*

Lewis was running down the stairs as if his life depended on it. No, not his—but Karissa's. He needed to find his wife. He heard a large commotion from behind him, but he figured that must've been the chapel falling apart. He hoped to god there would be a way out, otherwise he would be trapped in whatever hellscape he'd just entered.

After a few moments, the stairs led to a large door. As he went through, the first thing he noticed was a large white room. There were two dead Angels on the floor and a doctor with half of his face smashed into the wall.

*Jesus Christ, Bolton. What did you do?* the professor thought realizing this was the room where they created Angels.

He saw the state the doctor was in. It was almost as if an Angel had done it.

Lewis thought, *There is no way a human could do that, right?*

When he realized Bolton either went crazy or had become an Angel, Lewis quickly decided what to do next. There was another door on the other side of the lab. He looked around and grabbed a large knife from a table full of tools. He ran through the door and entered a hallway that looked as if it belonged to a hospital.

It was dimly lit and featured a few photos on the walls. They were of the scientist, Gunther. Some were just him alone, others with his creations. Lewis continued down the hall and noticed a red glowing light in the distance. It was a pulsating light, and it looked as though it was coming from the room to the right.

*What the hell?* Lewis thought.

It was absolutely silent. So silent that it made the red glow seem that much stranger. Lewis gripped the knife tightly, ready for anything.

He crept past the corner and saw two large glass doors. The red glow was coming from inside. Lewis opened the doors and walked in, and what he saw instantly gave him chills. There were large vats full of some kind of red liquid all over the place. Each vat held bodies. Some were large, some were small, some were women, and some were men.

Lewis had no idea what he was looking at, but he continued through the room, for all he cared about was Karissa. After a few moments, he noticed a door that would get him out of this room. Then he saw something out of the corner of his eye.

It was the source of the bright, pulsating red light. He slowly turned his head, and his eyes widened at the sight of it. He walked toward it. The red glow shined brightly as it reflected off of the sweat dripping down Lewis' head.

It was a metal capsule of some kind. It held a body. The body was pale and large. It was a male with an extremely good physique. Its eyes were wide open, and the corneas were a crimson red. It seemed as though, even though it looked awake, the body was in some sort of hibernation. His first thought was another Angel, but he quickly realized that no other body had been lit up or encased like this one.

No, this body was meant for something more.

But before Lewis could theorize more, the smell of smoke began to fill his nostrils. The fire began to burn down the stairs and into the hallways that led him to this discovery. He turned away and went out the other door. He figured if the whole lab was burning, the body and everything else would go with it.

He ran out the door and noticed some stairs that led up. Realizing it was most likely the way out, Lewis ran up them as fast as he could and didn't look back. Sure enough, the stairs led to a gate in the graveyard behind the chapel, which was now almost in ruins.

The snow was thick and steady. The wind was blowing mildly, but there were occasional and extremely powerful gusts. The fog was so thick, it was like walking into a wall of ice with every step. Lewis could barely see five feet in front of him, so he just looked down.

He then noticed different sets of footprints. Two were very large, like they belonged to Angels, and one was small and in between the larger footprints. He kept looking down and following the tracks. He could hear the screams of the villagers behind him. They weren't sad screams. They were angry, full of revenge and bloodlust.

He couldn't be bothered with that now. He needed to save the love of his life. The only love he'd ever truly known. The only thing that made him human. The only thing that kept him alive.

Karissa.

But something shocked him. A third set of footprints appeared. They were human sized. Lewis hoped to god it was Bolton, but after seeing the body in the basement—and remembering his own transformation into a Viking king named Artemis—he wasn't taking any chances. He took off as fast as he could while still being able to follow the tracks. Then he heard three gunshots in front of him.

"Karissa?!" Lewis yelled. He took off in a sprint, for his mind and body were filled with worry.

And fury.

*

About ten minutes before, Detective Andrew Bolton was running up the stairs from the lab that led to the chapel, which at this time was still somewhat intact. Gun in his hand and ready for anything, his fill of rage was rising. Rising so much that his will to escape lowered with every step, but his will to stay and kill every single member of the cult increased.

He wanted to kill them so bad.

He got to the top of the stairs and entered the chapel. Flames roared in front of him. Large logs separated him from the back room and the main room of the chapel.

Bolton had no other choice but to run out the back. There, he saw the snow beginning to fall. The fog was not yet fully upon the village, and he was able to see three figures moving up a hill: two very tall beings with a shorter one in between them. Bolton knew it would be the Angels and Karissa.

He began to move through the graveyard but was quickly grabbed from behind by some very large hands. Then he was thrown about fifteen feet, into the side of a house that sat next to the graveyard.

Bolton let out a grunt as he collected himself and looked up at his assailant. Sure enough, it was an Angel. This one's skin was gray, and its head featured long black strings of hair in different areas. Its eyes were large and wide open, as was its mouth, which was cut from ear to ear.

"Well, aren't you an ugly one," Bolton said, watching the angel move toward him as he attempted to get up. It took him a minute since he had just been thrown into a wall.

As he got about halfway to his feet, he quickly pulled out his gun and aimed at the Angel's head. But before he could pull the trigger, the tall gray being made one quick movement and swiped the gun away. It grabbed Bolton by the neck and lifted him up off his feet. It looked Bolton deep into his eyes, but he didn't turn away.

No, the detective looked right back into the Angel's face. He was remined of that fateful day. How scared he had been when all of his rage disappeared after he saw the Curry family dead on the floor. But was it relief that filled his mind after the killings, or was it the joy of revenge? Bolton felt so much rage and anger, he didn't care what happened. As far as he was concerned, everyone in that village was a member of the Curry family, and he wanted them all dead.

The Angel, still with its hand around Bolton's neck, was caught off guard when the detective put both his hands on the Angel's neck and began to squeeze. The gray Angel's eyes peered down to see the hands around its neck. Bolton, gasping for air due to the large hand around his own windpipe, was still staring into the Angel's eyes. A vein popping out of his forehead.

The Angel began to cough, then proceeded to throw Bolton into the side of the house he'd hit earlier. This time, Bolton actually went through the wall and into the house causing dust to fly into the air.

Bolton coughed and grabbed his neck as he tried to catch his breath. He looked at his hands and noticed they had black soot on them. He looked up and through the large hole in the side of the house. The gray Angel was still coughing. It looked confused. Sad, almost. When it looked up at Bolton, it had something strange on its neck.

Bolton had pressed so hard on the skinny gray neck of the Angel that his hands began to crush it. There was black ooze seeping out of its neck. Bolton used the confused state of the Angel to his advantage and ran out of the hole in the wall.

Running full speed and screaming like a banshee, he tackled the Angel to the ground. He looked the Angel in the eyes one last time before he proceeded to send a barrage of punches into the being's gray skull until it was nothing but a black gooey mash.

After the deed was done, Bolton sat back and sighed. There was black goop all over his hands and face. He looked up into the sky for a moment and enjoyed the snowfall. He always thought he'd been scared that day when he killed the Currys. But now he realized, when he looked back at the mess he'd made, he enjoyed it. He loved it, in fact. He eradicated the evil and that made him feel... good.

Bolton then stood up and began to walk toward the hill where Karissa was with the two Angels. He was not in a hurry. Not anymore. He picked his handgun up off the snowy ground and just kept going.

He thought about the fact that his whole life had been about the cult, he just didn't know it. The Currys were members of the cult, the members in the FBI were the ones who'd recruited him, and he was here now because of the cult. He had a wife and two daughters that he'd love to see more than anything. But in that moment, he believed it was only right to make the cult regret that they'd ever created who he became.

*

Karissa sat there on her knees, waiting. The leathery hands of the Angels gripped her shoulders. She prayed to whoever was listening that Lewis was still alive.

She remembered the day they bought their house in Portland. It was cloudy, just like usual, and Lewis woke her up with pancakes in bed that morning. He was so happy to move out of his apartment and into his life with her. Their real estate agent was extremely late to the closing, and while Karissa complained, Lewis smiled and cracked dad jokes. Karissa always thought of that memory as a bad one because they were supposed to move in by eleven that morning but didn't even get the keys until five that evening. Now, she was thinking of that moment like it was Heaven, and she would give anything to have it back.

Her fond memories were interrupted by the sound of a building collapse. It was the chapel, and she knew it. The last place she'd seen Lewis—the last place she may ever see her husband—had just collapsed into a pile of ash and cinder.

She screamed, "Lewis!" but was stopped short by an Angel slapping her, leaving her dazed. As she looked up, she saw a figure moving in on them. The fog was still so heavy, she could barely see anything but a shape. Plus, she was still recovering from the Angel's most recent blow. She could hear the bone-shattering screams of the villagers from down the hill.

Karissa could see the figure lifting up an arm. It was holding something. She squinted but couldn't make it out, until she saw a flash and heard a loud pop. Blood hit her face as the Angel to the right of her dropped instantly. The one on the left let her go and began to move quickly toward the figure, who then fired two more shots. Both bullets hit the body of the Angel, but it kept its fast-paced movement toward whoever was shooting. Karissa couldn't tell what was happening because both shapes collided in the fog.

But then, in an instant, the smaller one was thrown right toward her. It slid in the snow until it stopped at her feet.

It was Bolton.

"Hey, Karissa," he said, smiling through the pain.

"Andrew! Are you okay?" she responded, happily helping him back up onto his feet.

"Yeah, I'm good," he grunted as he watched the Angel walk toward him at a brisk pace. "We need to go, now."

Before Karissa could say a word, the Angel had his disgusting, bony hands on Bolton's neck. The tall being then lifted him up in the air. The detective tried to break the grip with his forearms but was unsuccessful. Karissa then tried to jump on the Angel's neck, but it was useless, as the Angel threw her off with one nudge of its back. It then walked a few steps forward, still holding Bolton by the throat, until it stopped. Andrew, struggling to move, was able to look down below him. Nothing but an abyss that would lead to a hard and fatal welcome from the rock and snow below.

The Angel was standing on the cliff.

Karissa charged at the being, not aware that she was only a few feet between solid earth and death. Bolton heard her feet in the snow and could tell she was running. He tried to yell at her to stop, but the bony hands of the Angel were crushing his windpipe. She was going to die and take them all with her. Bolton closed his eyes, preparing himself for what was below.

"Karissa!" a voice yelled.

Bolton's eyes opened wide. He saw the Angel turn its head back toward the village, and Karissa slid to a stop. Lewis appeared out of the white mist, holding a large knife. Karissa began to glow with excitement. A tear streamed down her cheek. But before any embraces were had, the Angel made a quick move, swung Bolton back on land, and forced him to his knees. Karissa was also within the Angel's grasp, and, sure enough, the deformity grabbed her and threw her on her knees next to Bolton in one quick motion.

"Whoa, whoa, whoa!" Lewis screamed with his hands up, as if he were telling the Angel to calm down.

The angel then pulled two large rusty daggers out from its robe and put one to the side of each of its captives' necks.

It began to make a repeated and terrifying noise. It sounded like somebody attempting to breathe during a heart attack, but Lewis knew it was a noise of victory.

The Angel believed it had won.

The professor gripped the knife in his hand and figured that the Angel would kill them both. He looked at Karissa, who was staring at him with watery eyes. Then he looked at Bolton, who was daydreaming about his two daughters and the family he left behind, wondering if the Cleansing had affected them at all.

And though the evil being's smile was permanently carved from ear to ear, Lewis knew it was actually smiling.

"Okay," Lewis said while lowering the knife. "You win."

"Lewis?" Karissa asked with wide eyes. "What are you doing?"

"Take me," Lewis said, dropping his head.

"Lewis!" Karissa screamed. "Stop, I can't lose you!"

"I'm sorry, Karissa," he said. "I really am. But I can't lose you either."

Lewis looked at Bolton with intent. It was a strange look, one that Bolton hadn't seen from Lewis before, but he knew what it meant. The detective understood and nodded his head.

"Bolton," Lewis continued. "I need you to look after her for me. Would you do that?"

"I will." Bolton said nodding his head.

Lewis slowly moved closer and closer to the Angel with his hands up in a non-threatening way. The Angel began to lower the rusty blades from their necks signaling it accepted Lewis' proposal.

"NOW!" Lewis screamed instantly jumping to a sprint toward the Angel. While the ghostly being began to slide the knives across its captives' necks, Bolton shot up and punched it square in its boney face. Lewis met the Angel at full sprint and lowered his shoulder. He was trying to truck the Angel off of the cliff. However, he was stopped short, as the Angel barely moved. Lewis bounced off of it and fell to the snowy ground.

"Shit," Lewis said, looking up in amazement.

Karissa was no longer in the Angel's grasp, and both she and Lewis turned to look at Bolton, who stood up and threw a punch that whipped the Angel's face around.

Then it slowly turned back to Bolton.

Lewis knew the detective needed some help, so he stood up, took off running, and tried the shoulder tuck again. This time, the Angel dodged it and sent Lewis sliding and then balancing on the edge of the cliff.

Karissa was looking around for anything that could help. She noticed Lewis' knife collecting snowflakes a few feet away and rushed to grab it.

Bolton received a hit with what felt like a sack of bricks to the face. The Angel cocked its arm back and hit him again; Bolton's mouth sprayed blood onto the snow. A punch to the gut by the Angel forced the detective to his knees. It then picked up one of the daggers it had dropped in the snow and cocked its arm back, ready to strike.

Lewis regained his balance and jumped on its deformed back, attempting to stop the attack on Bolton, who was battered and bruised. The Angel quickly thwarted his plan as it whipped its body, throwing Lewis into the snow. His head knocked on something, most likely a rock, and he began to bleed.

Karissa ran at the Angel with the knife. It dodged that attack as well and pushed her onto her back. Andrew Bolton stood up and attempted one more punch, but the Angel grabbed his arm.

It then proceeded to stab him in the abdomen, then dropped him onto his back in the snow.

"NO!" Lewis screamed, wiping blood from his forehead and standing up as fast as he could. It then pulled the knife out of Bolton and turned its attention to Lewis, who was charging it head-on.

The being hit Lewis with a swipe of its large hand so fast it sent him flying. Then it started after Lewis at a brisk pace and had no intention of slowing down. Lewis spit out some blood and looked the Angel in its soulless eyes. He knew his rage wanted out. But before it could be released, a knife entered the back of the Angel, and its stomach sprayed bile and blood all over the snow. Then the Angel turned around and noticed Karissa.

The knife was still in the Angel's back, so Lewis seized the opportunity and ran up to the tall being. He grabbed the knife, pulled it out, then proceeded to swing one final blow that was filled with rage, hate, and anger until the knife was lodged firmly in the side of the Angel's skull.

The tall being dropped. Its body was like a curtain that had stood between Lewis and his wife. And once it fell, they both looked at each other, then began to shed tears. But before they could embrace, they ran to Bolton, who was on his knees.

The snow around him was dark red.

Karissa helped Bolton lie down again. She knelt down on one side, and Lewis took the other.

"D-d-did you get the bastard?" Bolton said, stuttering. Blood streamed down the corner of his mouth.

Lewis nodded. "We did, buddy. We got him."

"Listen," Bolton said, struggling to get his words out. "You don't have a lot of time. That entire village is furious. You...you can hear them."

Sure enough, the Nelsons heard the continuous chanting of the villagers on their way up the hill. They looked down at Bolton, who said, "You gotta go."

"No!" Karissa said, tears streaming down her cheeks. "You're coming with us. We're going to get you out of here."

"I can't..." Bolton said.

"What about your family?" she asked. "They need you."

He shook his head and looked over at Lewis. "Listen, man. I'm sorry. For everything. I..."

Lewis cut him off. "Stop, Andrew. You are a great man. You do not need to apologize for anything. Your family knows you. They know how good of a father and husband you are. They will always know."

"We stopped this mess, Lewis. We really did."

"We sure did, buddy. And it was because of you. You saved us, and I thank you deeply for that." Lewis had a waterfall of tears falling from his cheeks.

Bolton grabbed Lewis' hand and looked at him in the eyes. "I need you to tell my wife what I did. Please. Tell my daughters who their dad was."

"Of course," Lewis said, choked up. "I'll make sure they know their dad was a hero."

"The treehouse, Lewis," Bolton said, closing his eyes. "The treehouse."

Lewis didn't understand. He looked at Karissa, who began to sob.

Bolton closed his eyes and imagined waking up to breakfast. His wife handing him his morning coffee and embracing him with a kiss. He was holding her in one arm and his coffee in the other as he watched his daughters play on the swing set outside of their house.

A moment of pure bliss.

And with that, Detective Andrew Bolton died in the arms of the Nelsons.

# ~ 12 ~

The rest of the world was in ashes. The Angels of Artemis continued to cleanse the world. Commissioner Byrd had just finished gunning down Agent Phil in the Portland streets, and now he was in his truck headed further downtown. His convoy of trucks was large and covered in spirals. Each one held a large machine gun in its bed.

Byrd had gotten a radio call from another group of cultists who needed some help fighting off a resistance. When he asked the cultist on the other side of the radio where they were, the transmission went quiet. So, he decided to head anywhere he could hear gunshots.

They were approaching a large bridge. Byrd continued to look around for any of his fellow cultists.

*BOOM!!!*

A large explosion behind them. One of the trucks in the convoy burst into flames, killing everyone inside.

Byrd's truck swerved off the road, hit the side rail of the bridge, and flipped over. It tumbled a few times and finally came to a stop on its side in the middle of the bridge. When he finally came to, a few cultists were trying to pull him out of the truck.

He then heard a barrage of gunshots—*very* loud gunshots.

Byrd was still trying to snap out of it. Then one of his fellow cultists was shot in the face, spraying blood all over.

He got ahold of his senses and began to crawl out the back window, where his arm got sliced on a piece of the truck and he let out a grunt. He held onto his arm and picked up the first gun he could find, which was a small handgun. He peeked over the truck and saw a group of cultists lying on the ground in pools of blood.

Every cultist looked as though they had been shot with a cannon. Some were missing limbs, and others were filled with holes the size of bowling balls.

Whoever was fighting back was using high powered weapons, and Byrd knew what that meant. It was either the military or the police. And since Byrd's group had wiped out most, if not all, of the police, it must have been the military. And, sure enough, when Byrd walked around the truck, he noticed some people in tan and camo uniforms coming straight for him.

At that very moment, an explosion from a grenade launcher sent Byrd flying back.

He tumbled a few times and grunted. As he attempted to get back up, he noticed the rest of his fellow cultists getting absolutely demolished.

Byrd looked around for an answer then looked down at his arm that was bleeding profusely.

"No, no, no!" He said and he watched the military group kill his last remaining allies. The military group then set their sights on him, guns aimed and loaded.

"Sir!" one of the soldiers said. "We got another one here!"

A man came up from behind the other soldiers. He pulled his goggles and mask off and looked Byrd right in his bloody eyes.

"Red robe," the man said. "He's a leader."

"Wait!" Byrd said, struggling to speak even a word. "How?"

"Aw," the man responded with a condescending tone. He walked over to Byrd and kneeled down in front of him. "You didn't hear? The world is fighting back against you scum. You're no more. Every single one of you showed yourselves, and that was your downfall."

"I don't believe it," Byrd stated. "We were supposed to cleanse all of you!"

It was Agent Bobby of the White Light task force. He proceeded to pull out his large handgun and aim it at Byrd's head.

"Well, believe it, prick," he said as he shot him in the face without hesitation.

Agent Bobby rejoined his team and headed off, attempting to find Agent Phil. And although Bobby would soon find out what happened to his friend, he took joy in knowing that Byrd died with the realization that he'd lost, that everything he and the rest of the cult worked for amounted to nothing.

Over the next twenty-four hours, the world's countries rallied their people and fought back against the Cleansing. Militaries stormed cities and killed every member of the cult they could find. Everyone fought dirty. They took no prisoners, and even civilians took up arms.

In about a day, the Cleansing was over. And while over forty thousand people ended up dead, the Angels of Artemis were no more.

The only followers left were over in Blackgate, with Karissa and Lewis Nelson, who were attempting to escape.

## ~ 13 ~

The villagers watched in horror as the chapel burned. Nobody ran away. Not even the children. Every single villager stood in sadness and anger. The bright orange glow from the flames could even be seen through the thickness of the fog and snow.

A few villagers heard a loud noise that sounded like a house falling apart. They thought it was the chapel being destroyed, but the sound had come from the left of the burning building. When one of them went to look, they noticed a dead Angel on the ground in a pool of dark black snow. The villager looked up toward the hill. A shadow was running into the fog.

The villager, a white bald man in his forties with a scar on his face, sprinted back to the fellow cultists to tell them what he had just seen. During this time, the chapel caved in on itself, leaving all of the villagers to scream in agony and rage. The villager with the scar on his face pointed toward the cliff.

At that moment, every single remaining member of the Angels of Artemis ran to their houses and grabbed any weapon they could find. Knives, machetes, axes, scythes, you name it.

Before they set off toward the cliff, they heard three gunshots coming from that direction. The bald cultist told the rest to follow him. They were going to avenge Calvin and the king himself, Artemis.

\*

Lewis looked down at his fallen friend. He was trying to come up with a way they could bring Bolton's body with them so he could give him a proper burial instead of letting him lie in this frozen hellscape. But no ideas came to mind. He and Karissa knew the cult would chase them off the end of the earth if they wanted to so, hauling a body through Iceland and onto a boat or plane would draw a lot of attention.

"I don't want to leave him here," Lewis said to his wife, who was kneeling right next to him.

"I know, Lewy."

"You know, I taught my students about grief. The emptiness, the large hole it throws you in. Nothing feels the way it should. The things that typically make you happy make you sad. The world becomes dark and gray."

"Lewis..."

"And although I am going to grieve the loss of a good friend..." He looked up into her eyes. "He led you back here to me. He saved our family and who knows how many others. And Karissa?" Now she looked at him in his eyes. "You are and have always been the love of my life. I will love you until the end of time, and I promise I will make everything up to you."

She shed a tear and smiled.

"I love you."

"I love you too."

They embraced each other and cried.

While the moment felt electrifying for them, it was cut short by the sounds of chanting creeping closer and closer.

Lewis grabbed her hand, and they stood up. They could see the orange glow of the villagers' torches.

"Okay, we have to get around them," Lewis said, looking in both directions. The cliff was the only thing he was afraid of. He then noticed that the large orange glow began to break up. The villagers were separating to cover more ground.

"Damn it."

"They know this land better than anyone, Lewis," Karissa started. "They know the outlines of the cliff."

Lewis agreed. "That leaves us one option."

Karissa stared at him in realization.

"We have to go through," he said, still trying to think of another option. But there was none. "Back to the village."

He grabbed Karissa by her hands. She felt how cold they were. "We'll use the snow and the fog to our advantage," he said. "They also have torches, so we will be able to see them from afar. And if any of them sees us, we run. Run as fast as we can. Okay?"

She nodded. Lewis gripped his knife tightly in his right hand.

Karissa's tears were freezing on her rosy red cheeks. There was no longer any time to show emotions. Survival was the only goal now.

Lewis led Karissa through the fog and closer to the villagers. Their chanting became louder and louder. The orange glow of the torches kept getting closer and closer. Fear rose up through the back of Karissa's spine. It was so chilling that the Icelandic snowstorm felt like summer in July.

After a few brief moments, Lewis told his wife to crouch down. They were nearing the first villager they needed to pass. They saw but a shadow of him, and his voice was deep and rusty. He chanted with a vengeance, and although neither of the Nelsons knew what he was saying, they knew that evil and revenge were behind it.

They waited for him to pass before slowly moving ahead. This time, there were three villagers in their way. Again, the Nelsons could not see them, only the orange glow of their torches and the sounds of the voices of those who held them. It was two women and one boy. His voice was high. Lewis figured he couldn't be more than thirteen. But even his voice was filled with rage.

The two women broke off and continued their path away. The boy continued to search the area around him, the area that was literally five feet away from the Nelsons. Lewis gripped the knife tightly, ready to strike. Karissa looked at him with wide eyes. She realized he was going to kill this boy. She knew it might be necessary, but thoughts poured into her mind.

Was he going to do it because he loved her? Because this cult had caused so much pain and suffering? Was he going to do it to avenge Bolton? One thing was clear to her: her beloved husband would do anything to get her home safe.

Thankfully, the little boy turned and ran toward the cliff because one of the villagers discovered the Angels' and Bolton's bodies. They screamed out, which led the rest of the villagers to swarm the area. The torches were moving so fast they looked like balls of fire zooming past the Nelsons' faces.

It offered them an open path around the village, and Lewis could not have been happier. However, that idea was scrapped because it wasn't long before one of the villagers yelled something loud in Icelandic and the balls of fire started to come straight for them. Lewis grabbed Karissa's hand and began to sprint straight to the village.

"They discovered our tracks!" Lewis yelled. "We gotta run!"

They sprinted through the graveyard that was behind the burned down church. Obviously, they couldn't go through the church anymore, so they headed to the right. There, they saw a dead Angel. His skin was gray and hideous. Above the dead being, they saw a house with a large hole in the side. They decided to go through there and collect their thoughts.

The villagers arrived at the graveyard and stopped. The Nelsons were crouched under the hole in the house, and Lewis put his finger up to his mouth. They listened intently as one villager said something. Lewis could tell they broke up and began searching, as the various sounds of feet in the snow either got louder (closer) or quieter (farther).

Lewis grabbed Karissa by the hand, and they began to crouch-walk toward the other side of the house. There was a wooden door there. He creaked the door open and peered out. There were villagers all around. The fog wasn't nearly as dense in the village as it was on the cliff, so that was another problem. Now, he had to lead his wife from house to house with numerous angry, evil villagers trying to find and kill them.

Or maybe something worse.

A few villagers passed down the main road through Blackgate. Lewis tracked them with his eyes and noticed they were going to the main gate. He looked up in the direction of the church and noticed most of the villagers were there. They were looking through the rubble of the church that was no longer on fire.

Seeking out survivors, Lewis thought.

He knew that in a matter of moments, they could find Calvin's dead body, which would cause the cultists to absolutely lose it. He knew he didn't have much time, so he made sure the alley behind the house was clear before he led Karissa to the next house. After another quick check, he went to the next house. Then the next one.

All of a sudden, a villager walked into the alley in the distance, which caused Lewis and his wife to slide in the snow and hide behind the house.

The villager heard the slide and began to walk toward the Nelsons. Karissa covered her mouth, as she was breathing heavily. Lewis listened intently to the sound of boots in the snow. They kept getting louder and louder. He gripped the knife hard and realized what he had to do. Once the sound of the boots seemed like it was upon the Nelsons, Lewis jumped out, knife ready to strike, and swung at the villager.

The only problem was that Lewis jumped out too early, and he only sliced the front of the man's robe. Both men looked down at the cut, and once they realized that it was only sliced fabric, they looked at each other. The villager opened his mouth wide, ready to scream, but Lewis seized the opportunity and penetrated the man's belly with the knife.

The only noise that came out of his mouth was a grunt. He stumbled into Lewis' arms until he pulled the knife out and did it again, this time in a much more vital area, which caused the man to fall down into the snow. Lewis knew he'd bleed out until he was found.

Karissa watched in horror as the man stared up into the sky with dead eyes. She looked at her husband. He was staring back at her. His hand reached out for hers.

She grabbed it, and they continued down the alleyway. In her mind, Karissa thought about how, for the past few weeks, she hadn't really been sure if her husband loved her anymore. Now, seeing everything play out and seeing him kill someone who could've killed them, there was no more wondering. He protected her at all costs. She knew it was her Lewy, her beloved, her soulmate. She held on to his hand tightly.

They were now close enough to see the gate.

Lewis stopped for a moment because the house they were at was the last bit of cover they could use. With the fog dissipating and the main gate about twenty feet away, they would need to make a run for it. Lucky enough, Karissa noticed something right outside the gate. It was the truck that she and Bolton had ridden into Blackgate.

"Lewis," she started, "Bolton and I drove here in that truck."

"Wait, really?" he asked with wide eyes.

She nodded her head. "There was a bag of guns in there as well."

Lewis' visible excitement started to fade. Once Karissa noticed and asked what was wrong, he said, "You don't by chance have the keys, do you?"

"No, I don't," she said, dropping her head. "And the bag of guns is probably gone by now."

"Well," Lewis started, "we either hope we don't get seen and run down to that town, which is pretty far away, so we could freeze to death, or one of these cultists could find us. Or we check the car and hope to god that the keys—or at least the guns—are in there. Or...we search the village for the guns or the keys and most likely die trying."

They looked at each other intently. They knew they were going to have to fight their way out either way. Lewis sighed and looked into his wife's eyes. "Okay look," he began, "I want you to sneak around these houses and look for the keys or the guns. I am going to run to the car, and if they are not there, I will create a distraction. This will lead the villagers away from you so you can have this whole place to yourself."

"No..." Karissa started, but he cut her off.

"If you find the keys, drive down the road and pick me up, because that's where I'll be. If you find the guns, I want you to load a few and shoot every single one of these bastards you see."

"And then find you, right?"

"If you only find the guns, I want you to think only about yourself. Find another way to leave this place, okay?"

"I'm not leaving you, Lewis," she said with tears streaming down her cheeks. "Not after I just got you back."

"I'm sorry, honey," he said, clenching his jaw. "I don't think we get to choose."

"Yes, we do," she said, grabbing his shoulder and pulling him close. "And I choose you. I'll always choose you."

They shared one final kiss before Lewis pulled away and said, "I love you." He leapt up and ran toward the front gate. As he was running, a few villagers noticed and began to chase after him. They started yelling, which of course caused the entire village to turn their attention to the front gates.

Karissa, still stunned from that move her husband had just pulled on her, shook her head and remembered the plan. She turned around and ran through the first house. It was dark in there. The only light came from embers in a firepit. She squinted and looked around. She checked an old wooden table and a hay-bale bed. Nothing.

Then she saw something. In the corner of the house was a long object. She reached out and felt the smooth wood and the hard metal. She picked it up.

It was a double barrel shotgun.

She clicked the lever and saw it was loaded. She looked around for any more ammo but couldn't find any. She kept searching but found nothing. Then her hand swept past a small sack. She quickly moved her hand back toward it until she felt it again and grabbed it. Once she opened the sack, the smell of gunpower hit her nostrils. Inside was about ten shotgun shells.

She then made her decision.

*

Lewis reached the car, but a villager tackled him into the snowy gravel. The rest were not far behind. The villager had a black mustache and a scar above his right eye that was leaking pus.

The man punched Lewis square in the chin, causing him to lose his breath. He recovered, though, and stopped the man's next attack with his forearm. He was reminded of his time in the chapel in Portland as the Angel jumped on him. Bolton shot it and saved Lewis that day.

However, today he was quickly reminded of Bolton's fate. He knew he had to get out of this situation himself. He focused and elbowed the villager in his gut, stunning him. Lewis used this time to reach for his knife, which lay under the tires of the truck, still within reach. He proceeded to swing the blade across the man's neck, leaving him a bloodied and gurgling mess.

He quickly threw the body off of him and sprang up to see another two villagers closing in on him. One had a pitchfork and attempted to stab Lewis. The charge missed, and the professor quickly grabbed the pitchfork and pulled it past him, which dragged the villager close enough for Lewis to stab him in the gut. Then he looked up at the next villager and took a quick peek to his right, inside the truck.

And, to his surprise, the keys were still inside.

They were sitting on the dashboard, just waiting for him and Karissa to shove them into the ignition and leave this nightmare behind. His eyes darted back to the next villager. This one was tall and skinny, not like an Angel. However, he was as close to a human as an Angel could get. He was holding a sickle, and his face was so bony it looked as though he was starving. Lewis bent his knees and readied his knife.

The man swung his sickle hard, and it nicked Lewis' arm. He let out a grunt of pain before spinning around and slicing through the man's robe. However, he was too skinny, and no flesh came away with that swing. The man used the professor's momentum against him and pushed him to the ground. Lewis looked up in fear as the man raised the sickle above his head.

But before he could bring it down and seal Lewis' fate, the villager's head exploded like a watermelon. The body fell onto Lewis, who then flipped it off of him in a hurry. He looked up and saw Karissa holding the double barrel shotgun, smoke still coming from the barrel.

"I told you," she said. "I'll always choose you."

He got up quickly and hugged her. "I love you," he said, kissing her passionately.

The rest of the villagers were getting closer, so Lewis hurried to the truck. "The keys are in here," he said.

Karissa ran to the other door, but when they both tried to open the truck, they realized the keys were locked inside. The villagers were now super close. Karissa turned around and aimed the shotgun at them as Lewis cocked his elbow back and hit the window.

It didn't break.

A villager came at Karissa, and she responded by blowing him back with a shotgun blast and a puff of red mist. She unclipped the barrel and loaded two more shells. Lewis cocked his arm again, and this time he was successful, and the glass broke.

He unlocked the door and got in. He reached over to Karissa's door and unlocked it.

"Get in!" he yelled at her.

She was finishing off another villager while Lewis grabbed the keys and put them into the ignition. The truck didn't start on the first turn of the key.

She shot another villager.

He turned the key again and heard the engine roar with power.

"Ah ha!" he yelled. He quickly noticed Karissa still wasn't in the car, and the wave of villagers was upon them.

"K, get in the damn car!" he yelled.

Out of ammo in the shotgun, Karissa flipped it around and hit another villager in the head with the butt. It slipped out of her hands after it made contact though, so she turned around and got right in the truck. Lewis began to speed off down the road until all of the villagers were no longer in their rearview mirror.

Both of the Nelsons sat quietly for a moment. Nothing could be heard but their heavy breathing and the engine of the truck that had just saved their lives. The cold air was blowing through Lewis' broken window, but neither of them cared. They had escaped the nightmare. Now the only thing to do was make it to town and find a way home.

Karissa turned her head to look at her husband. He had one hand on the wheel, the other on the gearshift. She put her hand on his. Both of them were blood soaked and smelled like death, but they were alive and, most important of all, together.

The road was iced over and the fog still heavy, but Lewis kept his eyes on the road and his grip on the wheel firm. No words were spoken between them on the drive. There was no need. After about twenty minutes, Karissa could see the town of Dalvik in the distance. They were driving down a long hill, and with every few feet things became clearer as the fog stayed in the mountains.

She could see the boats in the harbor and the bright colors of the buildings. Red, blue, and yellow. The lighthouse on the hill was a blazing red. The sun shined off of the ocean like glass. The closer they got, the more the smell of saltwater masked the stench of death.

It wasn't until they were about two miles away that Lewis said, "Check the glove box for a gun." As Karissa did, he continued, "We don't know if any of them are down here in town, so we have to be ready."

Well, the glove box didn't feature a handgun, but it did offer something else: a flare gun. There were two extra flares next to it. Karissa pulled it out and said, "This'll have to do. You still have your knife?"

Lewis nodded. The wind blew through his long brown hair. She hadn't had time to look at her husband in a while.

Not just look at him, but *really* look at him. Memorize his features, notice some wrinkles at the corners of his eyes. Notice how untamed his beard and hair had gotten. How black and blue his fingers were and the bruising on every inch of his body.

She wondered what it must've been like having somebody else inside his body and mind. Sharing a consciousness. She knew she was going to have to be there for him the way he was for her when this whole thing started. It must not have been easy or pleasurable.

They entered the town and instantly caught looks from other people. Was it because they came in speeding like bats out of hell? Or were their bloodstained clothes visible through the windows? It didn't matter.

Lewis drove them straight to the docks in search of a boat back to America. After they put the truck in park and got out, Karissa put the flare gun in the front of her jeans. The two extra flares went into her jacket pocket.

They walked toward a little yellow hut on the front of the dock. Inside was an old Icelandic man whose eyes widened at the sight of the couple.

"Hallo," the man said a bit hesitant, eying the two up and down.

"Hello, my name's Lewis," he started. "Do you speak English?"

The old man nodded and said, "How... can I help you two?" in an Icelandic accent.

"We need a boat back to America as fast as possible," Lewis said, wiping his forehead of sweat and blood.

"Well, we have one departing in about three hours." The old man looked both of the Nelsons up and down again. "Are you hurt?"

"No," Karissa said quickly. "But we are running from some very dangerous people, and we definitely need out before three hours, if you can."

The old man lowered his voice and checked his surroundings. "You come from the mountain?"

"Yes," Lewis said, dropping his head. "We know there are eyes everywhere, but we are just too tired to care anymore. If you can help us leave as soon as possible, it would mean a lot."

"A great evil lurks in these mountains and in this bay. A great evil I want no part of. I will get you two away from here." He reached into a drawer behind him and pulled out a set of keys. "My son's boat. It's the blue one at the end there." He nodded over his shoulder in the direction of the boat. "It is stocked with enough food and water for up to a month. However, I cannot promise that boat will make it back to America."

"You're just going to give us your son's boat?" Lewis said, creasing his eyebrows.

"My son is a part of that great evil, I'm afraid. It is more use to folks like you than it is to men like him."

"Thank you so much," Lewis said, grabbing the keys and making his way to the boat. The old man stopped them in their tracks and exited his hut. He walked close and spoke softly. "Understand that it is around a two-week journey to the port of New York. Also, I am not sure what your experience is out on the open waters, but nasty storms come through all the time without warning, so be careful." Lewis nodded, and the old man continued. "Another thing. I am not sure you are aware, but the great evil has spread its way around the world."

"What do you mean?" Karissa asked intently.

"The world is on fire, I'm afraid."

The Nelsons looked at each other in shock and disappointment. They then said their farewells and headed for the boat as the old man headed back to his hut.

It was a nice boat, one that could get them pretty far, but not far enough. That's exactly what Lewis said when he started it up and asked Karissa if she still had the flare gun, to which she replied yes. There was a bedroom on board with a drawer and a shower. Karissa set everything down and began to search the drawers.

Sure enough, there were a few sets of clothing. Some very big, as if they had been made for a large or possibly obese person. And some were small, most likely belonging to a petite woman.

Lewis began to drive the boat away from the harbor while his wife exited the bedroom holding piles of clothes. They both turned around and said one final farewell to Iceland and a hello to whatever they would be coming home to.

*

A few hours later, Lewis turned off the motor for a bit. The wind was blowing in the direction they were headed, so he thought they could save some fuel and let the current take them as far as it could.

Karissa had showered and was sitting next to the shower door while Lewis finished up.

"Hey," Lewis said from inside the shower. "How did you learn to use a gun like that?"

His wife was drying her hair with a towel. "My dad was always worried about other men when I was growing up. He taught me how to defend myself. I never told you, I guess because it never seemed important."

"Hm," Lewis said, pleasantly surprised. His wife had saved his life, and he was grateful.

After they were both showered and clothed, Lewis trimmed his beard with an electric razor he'd found in the bathroom while Karissa examined the flare gun.

She had on a red long-sleeved tee and black leggings, while Lewis had on an oversized brown flannel and some very large jeans that even a belt was struggling to keep up.

When Karissa saw her husband in this outfit, she couldn't help but laugh. Lewis looked upon her with a smirk and said, "Oh, that's funny, huh?"

Her smile quickly became faint, and she looked at her husband with wet eyes. He gave her the same look until the first tear streamed down her cheek. Once Lewis saw that, he darted over to her and held her tightly. They both began to sob in each other's arms. They were now able to feel the weight of every little thing that had happened to them.

The professor thought about his life before all this. Every morning, coffee and kisses from his wife and dog. Then to the university to teach students about the criminal justice system and those who had to face it. Those who deserved justice.

Karissa thought about her life, which would never be the same. She thought about the amazing news her boss had given her when she was awarded the big news story. In a matter of weeks, she would see her dog killed, go on an incredibly terrifying journey, and witness her husband become somebody else entirely.

She cried harder. Lewis held her tightly and said, "You saved me, you know that?"

She looked up into his watery eyes. "I wasn't strong. I..."

He stopped her. "Karissa, you are the strongest woman I've ever met. You saved my life and the lives of countless others. You did what you said you would do; you kept going north."

She kissed him passionately as the waves carried them further toward their destination. They embraced each other with so much love, it felt like the whole world had stopped turning. They were together now and forever.

After few days, the Nelsons used the flare gun to signal a cargo ship, which was on its way to America. Once they were on board, the ship's captain explained what had happened to the world. Cultists who had been embedded in society had shown themselves and attempted to "cleanse" the world. When the captain said that nobody knew why, both of the Nelsons just looked at each other.

The captain went on to say that some task force from the FBI, White Light, was wiping out the rest of the cult members while the government was cleaning the streets. When the captain told them that Chicago, Los Angeles, and Portland were hit the hardest and that there was pretty much nothing left of those cities, they both looked down in sadness, and Lewis gripped his wife's hand.

Around forty thousand people were killed and one hundred thousand were still missing. The Angels of Artemis had completely shaken the world. However, it was already starting to make a comeback. The usual corporate greed was nowhere to be seen, as new CEOs and board members were sending money worldwide in efforts to help. Food shelters were sprouting up all over the place, memorials were being held for free, and churches offered housing to those who were now homeless. It was a whole new world of peace and hope. While rubble and debris still filled the streets, there was beauty in the people, in their will to survive and keep moving.

\*

Karissa and Lewis went back to Portland to see what was left of their lives. Their house was still in one piece, but once they figured out that Lisa Garcia was dead and that her husband Jack had been a part of the cult, they packed up and left.

Seattle wasn't hit nearly as hard as some other cities, and they had actually cleaned up pretty quick. Once Lewis found a house that was out of the city limits but still close enough to civilization, they moved in.

\*

A few weeks later, on a rainy night, Lewis was brushing his teeth, getting ready to watch the Oregon football game. Their new German shepherd puppy was sitting on the bed with his head cocked to the side, wondering what his owner was doing.

Karissa walked in wearing an Oregon T-shirt and baggy pajama pants. The smell of pizza still lingered from the kitchen.

Lewis said, "What's up, K?" with a mouthful of toothpaste.

She stood in the doorway and cracked a smile. Her cheeks began to turn bright red. Lewis looked at her with wide eyes and immediately stopped brushing his teeth.

"I'm pregnant."

Lewis dropped his toothbrush, instantly picked up his wife, and spun her around. She laughed and laughed until her husband put her down and continuously kissed her.

She broke away and said, "Ah, you're getting toothpaste all over me!"

"Well, now you don't have to brush your teeth," he said jokingly. They spent the rest of that evening enjoying football and each other. The Nelson's were getting back to their lives.

# ~ 15 ~

About two months had gone by. Lewis was packing a suitcase into his car as Karissa watched, hand on her belly. The sun had just risen, and the clouds were scattered. A cold breeze was in the air.

He walked up to his wife and gave her a hug and a kiss. "You sure you're going to be okay without me for a couple of days?"

"I'll be fine, Lewy," she said, smiling. "A few of the girls are coming over to keep me company."

"I can stay if you want," he said with a concerned look.

"No, baby. You need to go," she replied. "They need this."

Lewis nodded and got in his car. As he was backing out of the driveway, he rolled down the window and yelled, "Better not get famous while I'm gone!"

She waved him off and then blew him a kiss. Lewis watched in the rearview mirror as she walked back inside.

He then headed to the airport.

Once he got there, he checked his bags and went through security. He was checking his emails at the gate when he opened one that said "Congratulations!" from the University of Seattle.

\*

When he exited the airport, Lewis could feel the heat and humidity in the air—much different from Seattle's cool and rainy climate. The professor made his way to the rental car area and proceeded to get a nice large black truck. He thanked the nice old lady who stood behind the counter, and she replied with, "You're welcome, honey," in a Southern twang.

Lewis began his journey by hopping on the highway and thinking about his life. About how he was going to be a father. About how had Karissa scored the story of the century, which without a doubt would get her the recognition she had always wanted. About how he'd be teaching criminology at the University of Seattle. He continued to think about how good things were going as he headed down the highway until he reached an exit that led to a small town.

The town was at the bottom of a mountain and only had one main street. The rest of the streets led to houses that sat on the outskirts or in the hills. As he drove though, almost every single person he passed, whether they were in a car or walking down the street, greeted him with a smile and a wave.

Lewis got to the other side of town and made a left toward a wooded area. Trees with red and yellow leaves began to take the place of old buildings, and Lewis could feel a slight breeze in the air. He continued down this road until he reached a nice red suburban house.

He parked out front and took in the details. It had a well-kept front yard and featured a great big tree that was standing strong like a guardian. Lewis noticed the tree had some swings hanging from it, and two little girls were playing. He also noticed the beginnings of a treehouse on one of the branches.

When the two little girls noticed Lewis, they went inside to inform their mom. He started to get out of the car as a thin blonde woman walked out the front door. She was dressed in a sweater and had a look of curiosity on her face.

"Can I help you?" she said, standing close to her house.

"Mrs. Bolton?" Lewis asked with a clinched jaw. His throat was tightening.

"Yes?" she replied.

Lewis walked up and introduced himself. He reached into his pocket and pulled out a small gold ring. Once she saw it, she broke down crying and hugged Lewis.

Back on that cliff at Blackgate, he'd realized that that ring would be the only piece of her husband she could get back. The FBI had contacted the Boltons about three days after Lewis and Karissa got back from Iceland. They wouldn't be able to return Andrew's body. Once Lewis heard that news, he knew he needed to give his wife some form of peace.

Lewis held her in his arms and said, "I know I can't give you much, but I want you to know that your husband saved my life. He will always be remembered as a hero and a friend."

Mrs. Bolton wiped her eyes and said, "Thank you." Then she invited him inside for some tea and dinner.

That night, Lewis and the Boltons shared stories of Andrew while the sun went down over a kind and beautiful

Tennessee sky. Lewis said he was going to help finish building the treehouse for Bolton's daughters. The evil had been defeated, and all that was left to do was rebuild and keep going north.

# ~ 16 ~

## EPILOGUE

The ashes mixed in with the snowflakes as they fell. The fire in the village left the church in ruins of stone and soot. Villagers were scattered. Some were on their knees, sobbing over their fallen friends and family. Some were watching the smoke fade off into the clouds. Others were pulling stones from the ruins.

There were a few men whose black robes looked gray from stains of ash. They were pulling rubble and debris from one particular area. One man was tall and had a long beard, while the other two were short and stocky. Each one was bald. No words were spoken between the men, not even when one of them pulled down the last piece of wood that sat over a doorway.

The doorway led down a large stairway. The entire hall was black and burned but still standing. The three men continued until they reached what seemed like a lab. There were a few burned remains of people on the floor. Two of them were obviously fallen Angels.

The men continued to roam the burned hallways, which still held plumes of smoke, until they reached another large room. There, about half of the walls were caved in. After sharing a look and a nod with the other two, the taller man left the room, and the others began to clear debris.

After about ten minutes, the tall villager walked back in with shovels in both his hands. He handed one to one of the shorter villagers, and they began to dig. They had to be very careful, as they knew even a small piece of debris could be holding up the entire room.

After an hour of slow and careful digging, one of the short men, the one without the shovel, lifted up a large stone. As soon as he did a bright red light shined through, hitting them all in the eyes. They all shared a look of excitement once they bore witness to what lay beneath that rubble. It was a metal container holding a body. The red light shined from behind the body—the experiment was still on. The look on the villagers' faces indicated that what they'd found meant anything but the end of the Angels of Artemis.

# ABOUT THE AUTHOR

Cal Neubert graduated from CSU-Pueblo in 2021 with a degree in Mass Communications with an emphasis in journalism. After excelling as a student athlete most of his life, he was struck with a career-ending injury in 2019. After having to leave the sport he loved so much, Neubert lost his way.

He changed his major, stayed inside every day, and stopped caring about his physical health. His sister, Tatum Neubert, had eventually told him he should start writing his thoughts in a journal. Cal listened to his older sister and began writing in his journal daily.

The daily writing developed into poetry, which then grew into short stories, which then strengthened into his first novel, The Cleansing.

With his newfound passion for writing fiction novels, Neubert doesn't plan on slowing down anytime soon. Already finished with the first story in a planned trilogy, you can expect to see Neubert's work evolve over time.

None of the events that take place in this book nor the characters are real. All locations, businesses, and universities are either made up or are strictly used for literation purposes.

9 781088 055106